BAD BILLIONAIRES QUICKIES

BILLIONAIRE'S CLUB NOVELLAS

ELISE FABER

BAD BILLIONAIRES QUICKIES
BY ELISE FABER

Newsletter sign-up

BAD BILLIONAIRES QUICKIES
Copyright © 2021 Elise Faber
Print ISBN-13: 978-1-63749-026-6
Ebook ISBN-13: 978-1-63749-025-9
Cover Art by Jena Brignola

BILLIONAIRE'S CLUB

Bad Swipe

BILLIONAIRE'S CLUB CAST OF CHARACTERS

Heroes and Heroines:

Abigail Roberts (Bad Night Stand) — founding member of the Sextant, hates wine, loves crocheting

Jordan O'Keith (Bad Night Stand) — Heather's brother, former owner of RoboTech

Cecilia (CeCe) Thiele (Bad Breakup) — former nanny to Hunter, talented artist

Colin McGregor (Bad Breakup) — Scottish duke, owner of McGregor Enterprises

Heather O'Keith (Bad Husband) — CEO of RoboTech, Jordan's sister

Clay Steele (Bad Husband) — Heather's business rival, CEO of Steele Technologies

Kay (Bad Date) — romance writer, hates to be stood up

Garret Williams (Bad Date) — former rugby player

Rachel Morris (Bad Hookup) — Heather's assistant, superpowers include being ultra-organized

Sebastian (Bas) Scott (Bad Hookup) — Devon Scott's brother, Clay's assistant

Rebecca (Bec) Darden (Bad Divorce) — kickass lawyer, New York roots

Luke Pearson (Bad Divorce) — Southern gentleman, CEO Pearson Energies

Seraphina Delgado (Bad Fiancé) — romantic to the core, looks like a bombshell, but even prettier on the inside

Tate Connor (Bad Fiancé) — tech genius, scared to be burned by love

Lorelai (Bad Text) — drunk texts don't make her happy

Logan Smith (Bad Text) — former military, sometimes drunk texts are for the best

Kelsey Scott (Bad Boyfriend) — Bas and Devon's sister, engineer at RoboTech, brilliant

Tanner Pearson (Bad Boyfriend) — Bas and Devon's childhood friend, photographer

Trix Donovan (Bad Blind Date) — Heather's sister, Jordan's half-sister, nurse who worked in war zones, poverty-stricken areas, and abroad for almost a decade

Jet Hansen (Bad Blind Date) — a doctor Trix worked with

Molly Miller (Bad Wedding) — owner of Molly's, a kickass bakery in San Francisco

Jackson Davis (Bad Wedding) — Molly's ex-fiancé

Kate McLeod (Bad Engagement) — Kelsey's college friend, advertiser extraordinaire, loves purple and Hermione Granger

Jaime Huntingon (Bad Engagement) — vet, does excellent man-bun

Heidi Greene (Bad Bridesmaid) — science, organization, and *Twilight* nerd

Brad Huntington (Bad Bridesmaid) — travel junkie, dreamy hazel eyes, hidden sweet side

Additional Characters:

George O'Keith — Jordan's dad
Hunter O'Keith — Jordan's nephew

Bridget McGregor — Colin's mom

Lena McGregor — Colin's sister

Bobby Donovan — Heather's half and Trix's full brother

Frances and Sugar Delgado — Sera's parents

Devon Scott — Kels and Bas's brother

Becca Scott — Kels and Bas's sister in law

Cora Hutchins — Kels' friend since childhood

BAD DATE

CHAPTER ONE

Kay

"Go on a blind date, they said. It will be fun, they said."

Kay sighed and slumped back into her chair. Nothing like sitting alone for over an hour at the very expensive and chic restaurant her date had insisted upon. She was way outclassed at Ange Bisou and had only agreed to meet there in the first place because she was trying to force herself to step out of her comfort zone.

Routines were her mojo.

In fact, she loved nothing more than following them to a tee.

Which was probably why she was still single.

Ugh.

Kay pull out her phone, as if glancing at it for the hundredth time in the last hour might make a call or text magically appear, as if looking at it might mean she hadn't actually been stood up . . . for a date she hadn't wanted to go on in the first place.

Frankly, she had a hard time thinking that *any* date could possibly be worth her having to change out of her daytime pajamas and into actual adult clothes.

Yes, her normal routine involved daytime pajamas.

She stared at her phone, irritated all over again, because right about now—eight forty-five—she should be finishing up her bath and changing into her sleep pajamas. Maybe with a glass of chardonnay and definitely with a cooking show streaming on Hulu.

Not that she could cook.

Nope. Kay could burn water.

But lack of cooking skills aside, she still enjoyed watching what those chefs could whip up.

Plus, one of her favorite chefs had worked at Ange Bisou. So, despite her having to get out of her pajamas and her routine being completely obliterated, she'd actually been looking forward to eating here tonight.

Until she'd found herself sitting at the table alone.

Kay wished she'd ordered something earlier, but it was too late. She was already an hour in and nursing her second glass of wine, though she *had* given into the urge to get busy with the bread basket ten minutes ago.

She should have ordered the beet salad.

That was Christie's addition to the menu. And, yes, she considered herself on a first name basis with her fave celebrity chef, because watching every episode of a reality cooking competition meant they'd become friends, right?

Well now, *that* was a little slice of pathetic.

Sighing, she caught the waiter's eye.

"Can I get you anything else?" he asked, his gaze deliberately on her face and not the empty chair or unused flatware on the other side of the table.

She shook her head. "Just the bill. Thank you."

"Sure thing."

Kay shoved another bit of bread into her mouth as she waited, watching as the patrons around her ate *coq au vin* and chocolate soufflé.

Oh, good God. They had chocolate soufflé.

Her eyes rolled to the ceiling and she forced herself to

breathe. She wished she had the guts to say fuck it all and order dinner, to sit and enjoy it.

But she knew herself.

She'd order the beet salad and the chocolate soufflé, and then she would be miserable and self-conscious eating them by herself.

And this didn't seem like the type of place to pull out a book as a shield.

Nope.

Plus, even if it was, it didn't matter. Because Kay was ready to go home, ready to change into her sleep pajamas and watch repeats of *Great British Bake Off*. They gave her hope that someday she might actually develop some cooking chops . . . instead of cooking *pork*chops into submission.

Because shoe leather had nothing on hers.

Her gaze drifted to the other table, the one with the chocolate soufflé. The woman who'd ordered it had only eaten half and then she nodded to the waiter when he asked if she'd finished.

What kind of monster only finishes half a soufflé?

Kay's nose wrinkled and her inner voice turned all grumbly. She wished *she* had a soufflé. She wouldn't waste it.

And—*ugh*—because *now* the woman reached across the table and her partner or date or husband also stretched his hand out to lace their fingers together, his other palm coming up to cup her cheek. It was sweet and lovely and romantic—

"I want to be home," she whined under her breath. "Right now."

Romance was dead for the romance writer.

How fitting.

Blinking, she dug out her wallet and by the time her waiter returned with her check, she was ready, all but tossing her card onto the little metal tray. He zipped away and back in record time and then she scrawled her name, paying fifty bucks for two glasses of wine and a tip to make the poor guy's night worth it.

Probably not as much as he would have made if she and her nonexistent date had actually eaten, but he'd been nice and not judgy, and hopefully it would take the edge off.

It wasn't his fault that she'd been stood up.

Nope. That particular responsibility lay solely in Garret's lap.

Kay blew out a breath, shrugged into her coat, and picked up her purse. The only good news was that her sleep pajamas were ready and waiting for her, laid out on her mattress.

She strode out of the restaurant, smiling to the hostess as she pushed through the door, and had just turned in the direction of her car when—

Wham!

Her purse dropped to the ground, spilling its contents everywhere, and she stumbled, almost falling, as a man shoved past her, cell phone glued to his ear.

He paused, glanced downing at her as though surprised to see a peon such as her existed. Probably not fair since there was a trace of concern in his gaze, but she certainly felt like a peasant when compared to the god in front of her.

Tall, dark, hot.

Black hair with the barest hint of a wave, tan skin and deep chocolate eyes, a jawline that could have been chiseled out of marble.

Yup. He was easy on the eyes.

"You okay?" he asked, and her heart skipped a beat.

Maybe not *all* men were assholes.

"I'm—" she began.

But once again, optimism was proven wrong.

Tall, dark, and handsome didn't wait for her answer. Whoever was on the phone must have snagged his attention, because his expression hardened and he turned away, saying, "I don't care if I'm late—"

Pieces fell into place.

Garret Williams, her MIA date, was a former rugby player from Australia. He'd recently begun a project with one of Heather's subsidiaries.

Heather O'Keith was an accidental friend—more about that later—and had been pestering Kay about setting up this date for months.

Garret was tall.

Garret was built.

Garret had the most gorgeous chocolate eyes Heather had *ever* seen.

Kay's own eyes flicked back to the man, who was now yanking open the door. Check. Check. Check.

"—You know I didn't even want to do this in the first place."

She'd been expecting an Australian accent, considering he was from Australia, but he sounded American. Well, chalk it up to things she would never know.

The door shut, cutting off anything else he might have said, and leaving Kay alone on the sidewalk, purse's contents strewn in all directions, and temper rapidly rising.

"Stupid"—she grabbed her book, shoved it back into her bag—"men."

Then Kay snatched up her keys, wallet, lipstick, pack of gum, two hair ties, and a few bobby pins and tucked them into her purse, all while muttering under her breath about the irritating creatures of the opposite sex who were hot but didn't appear to give a damn about anyone but themselves.

What the fuck had Heather been thinking?

You know what?

What had *she* been thinking?

Letting that asshole crash into her with nary an apology, allowing him to leave her to crawl across the dirty sidewalk gathering up her personal items. She hadn't even managed to say anything useful, just been blinded by his gorgeous god-like-ness and had let him traipse off like a big ole'—

Ugh.

Like a big ole' something that was really insulting and annoying and—

The door opened again, a man holding it wide for his wife. Kay probably would have left at that moment, gone back to her apartment to sulk in peace, *if* the tall, dark, and handsome man she assumed was Garret Williams hadn't still been in the lobby of the restaurant. But nope, he was still there, still on his phone, still talking loudly enough that she could hear every single word through the open door.

And what she heard took her temper from bubbling to boiling.

"What kind of woman writes romance novels anyway?" he said. "She's probably an awkward cow who'll just stare at me through giant glasses the whole time I'm eating."

Kay's jaw dropped open. Her hand snatched at the door handle when it started to close.

He chuckled and said, *"Exactly,"* like the snarky little asshole he was.

A vision of a pot boiling over filled her mind, or maybe a tea kettle whistling as steam poured out its spout. Either way, all Kay knew was that she saw literal red as she stormed back into the restaurant.

Just as she approached him, he hung up the phone, tucking it into his pocket and opening his mouth.

"Garret Williams?" she asked.

Furious as she was, she'd managed to hold on to enough reason to make sure the man she was about eviscerate was, in fact, her absentee date.

He rotated to face her. "Yes?"

She reached into her purse, yanked out a paperback of her latest release. She'd intended to give it to Heather when they met up for coffee tomorrow, but this was more important. Plus, Heather had already read the ebook. The paper version had just been intended as a thank you for being awesome and a good friend and—

Right now that didn't matter.

Kay slapped the book against Garret's chest. The action made a satisfying *smack*, especially when she pretended it was actually her hand making contact with his cheek.

But first, he was so tall she couldn't reach it without a ladder.

And second, she didn't want to be arrested for assault.

Yeah. Minor details.

"What's this—"

She narrowed her eyes and took great joy in cutting him off. "Only your *cow* of a date's latest release. Maybe you should check the *New York Times* the next time you go searching for your decency."

He winced, looked the slightest bit sick. "Katherine?"

Kay lifted her chin, huffed dismissively, and followed up with an insult she would later look upon with pride. For once, she hadn't rolled over and accepted some asshole's judgment. She'd owned him *and* the situation.

"I go by Kay."

A beat.

"But in your case, I go by Fuck-Off-Because-You-Never-Even-Had-A-Chance."

And she walked out of the restaurant.

There should have been trumpets and banners . . . or at the very least, a round of applause as she went.

Instead, the only thing that trailed her was the *click-click* of her heels.

But, for that night, it was enough.

CHAPTER TWO

Kay

"JUST BECAUSE YOU saved my laptop from that Venti Frappuccino doesn't mean you get to torture me," she accused Heather the following day. She flopped down into the chair across from her friend. It was a dramatic move, but Kay held on to enough sense to not spill the steaming cup of tea she'd just purchased.

Her friend winced and took a sip of her coffee. "I'm guessing things didn't go well last night?"

"Well?" Kay snorted. "An unmitigated disaster would be a more accurate description."

"Damn, did he talk about himself too much?" Heather asked. "Sometimes people get nervous and try to impress their dates. Or was he too accommodating? Like he was so worried about you and your feelings that you didn't get to know him at all?"

"Heath," Kay replied. "I'm saying this with the utmost affection but . . . you're losing your touch. Your wonderful hubby has rotted your once sharp and precise brain." She raised a finger when Heather would have argued. "I see it with my characters all the time. They fall in love and they get soft—"

"One," Heather interjected. "Your characters are a product of your brain, so they don't get full human status in this argument and two, RoboTech and its subsidiaries made record profits last year, so my hubby isn't making me soft. Rather"—she waggled her eyebrows—"he's giving me *hard*."

"First," Kay said, mimicking her, "gross. And second . . . gross."

"That's all you got?" Heather lifted a brow. "I thought you were supposed to be some super successful author."

Kay rolled her eyes. "Words are hard."

Heather's mouth curved. "Uh-huh. Okay, so why was your date with Garret a disaster?"

"Before or after he stood me up?"

Kay had to hand it to herself, she'd surprised her friend and *that* didn't happen very often. So, she took great pleasure in the slack-jawed expression currently adorning Heather's face.

"I waited an hour," she said. "Nursed that bread basket like a son of a bitch, downed two glasses of really good wine. But after sitting alone at the table for an hour, I decided I'd had enough punishment and so I paid and left."

Heather winced. "Shit. I'm so sorry. I thought Garret was—"

"I haven't even got to what happened *after* the date ditching."

"Hold on"—Heather took a slug of coffee—I need to prepare myself. Especially since I'm the one who forced you to go out with him." She sucked in a breath, released it. "Okay, go."

"He called me a cow."

The look on Heather's face was scary, Kay had to give her friend that much. *And* it wasn't even directed at her, so really, she hadn't even witnessed the full potential of that glare.

"He. Did. *What?*"

Kay explained leaving the restaurant, the sexy—albeit awful—man who'd knocked into her, causing her to spill her purse, before overhearing the conversation and—

"Then he basically said only gross cows write romance

novels and that he'd purposely come late because he didn't want to be there in the first place." Kay sipped her tea. "And so I walked over to him, slapped him in the chest with one of my books, and walked out."

"You didn't!" Heather gasped.

Kay nodded. "Fuck yes, I did."

"That is amazing," Heather said, and the slight awe in her tone smoothed over the ruffled edges of Kay's temper. "You should have really slapped him though."

Kay sighed and sat back. "As much as I wanted to, you know how I feel about actual violence."

"You and your morals."

"I know"—Kay's lips twitched—"pesky standards."

Heather's phone buzzed, but she kept her eyes on Kay's. "I'm really sorry. Garret mentioned to Clay that he was single and looking to settle down, but that he'd been struggling to find smart, talented woman, I thought, *Who's smarter and more talented than you?*"

Aw.

Another buzz, which Heather ignored. "Obviously, I knew you fit the bill, but I didn't know he'd be such a douche. Next time—"

"There will be no *next time*, Heather O'Keith." Kay narrowed her eyes.

Heather's phone buzzed for a third time, and she sighed. "I need to go."

"Not until you promise no more blind dates."

Avoiding Kay's eyes, she stood up, tossed her purse over one shoulder and turned to leave. "It was good to meet up. I can't wait for your next book!"

"No more new books unless you agree to no more blind dates."

Heather winced. "You're mean."

"I'm practical. That was torture, and I'm old enough to only want to do things that *I* want to do." All well and good in words, but Kay had serious pushover tendencies, which Heather certainly knew . . . and would probably exploit if the chips were on the table.

"It's for your own good," Heather began.

See?

"I'm happy with my life," she told her. "Would I turn the right man away if he dropped into my lap? Hell no. But I'm not actively looking for a relationship, and I'm totally fine with that."

"But you're a romance writer," Heather said. "You create stories that make people happy, and you deserve to have some of that happy for yourself."

Kay smiled and pushed to her feet. "Thank you for caring." She hugged Heather. "But I *am* happy and if you read some of my reviews, you'd see that I make plenty of people miserable." Her smile widened to a grin. "Plus, consider this whole horrible event fodder for my new book. I'll name someone Garret, kill him off, and then move on with my life in blissful abandon."

Heather considered that for a few seconds. "Okay, fine." She finally glanced down at her cell and made at face at what she saw on the screen. "I just don't understand how he transformed from Mr. Nice Guy into Sir Asshole."

"Either way," Kay said. "He's not Mr. Right. So"—and she wanted to make this crystal clear because Heather was a master negotiator and had a penchant for finding workarounds and loopholes—"repeat after me: No more blind dates."

Her friend nodded. "No more setting you up on blind dates. Got it."

And with a quick squeeze and a promise of dinner soon, Heather left.

Kay stared after her, trying to figure out why that interaction had come off as weird. Heather's agreement had been almost too easy, but then again, she *had* felt bad about the disaster of a date, so maybe that was it.

Huh. Kay shrugged mentally as she pulled out her laptop.

Weirdness aside, Heather was a woman of her word. If she promised no more blind dates, she would follow through with that.

It was only later that Kay would realize that while Heather had promised no more blind dates, what she *hadn't* promised was to forgo dates altogether.

Words, man. Sometimes they came back and bit a girl on the—

CHAPTER THREE

Garret

HE'D KNOWN he'd fucked up from the moment he'd watched the beautiful blonde come his way, pretty chocolate eyes molten and all but shooting sparks.

Garret knew he'd pissed her off, but hadn't comprehended why.

Had he broken something when he accidentally bumped into her?

He knew he probably should have stopped to help her pick up her things, to make sure she was fine, but he'd already been late and wanting to get the evening over with.

Not to mention the rant. He'd been spouting off to his best friend and former teammate, Kevin, like he'd earned a gold medal in ranting.

But then the woman had approached with fury written across her face, and so Garret had quickly hung up his call, pocketed his cell, and opened his mouth to apologize. But he hadn't managed to get more than a syllable out before she was assaulting him with a paperback and then telling him to check out the *New York Times* listings.

And *that* was the precise moment he realized the degree to which he'd fucked up.

Because the beautiful blonde wasn't just a stranger he'd bumped into on the street.

Nope. She was his date.

A date he hadn't wanted, but one that had been his investor's idea. Heather O'Keith was a legend in the business world, and when she'd found out he was single and potentially looking for that status to change, she'd all but forced one Katherine Hart on him.

What was he going to say? No?

Of course not.

He wanted RoboTech's investment, and he was counting on Heather's business acumen.

So he'd agreed to the date.

But inwardly, he'd groaned and moaned and bitched as if his coach had dressed him down in front of the guys. And this inner whine-fest had only grown louder when Heather told him how she'd met Katherine and that her friend was a romance novelist.

First, Garret was a realist. He didn't have room in his life for someone who spent time fantasizing over fictional eight-packs and happy endings that rarely came to fruition.

Second, he'd pictured a woman who looked like those from the backs of his mother's books. Bodice rippers still cluttered her nightstand and, well, this was going to make him sound like a Class-A asshole again, but the women whose pictures were on the back of those hadn't exactly been his type. They appeared a little frumpy, slightly awkward, and old enough to be his . . . *well*, his mother.

Of course, what he *hadn't* expected was tall, lean, and gorgeous with angelic features and lush lips that any man would dream of kissing. Even her glasses had added to her allure.

Katherine—or Kay as she'd told him she went by—definitely had the sexy librarian vibe happening.

And if there was one thing that Garret dug, it was the sexy librarian look.

Contrary to his size as an adult, he'd been little growing up. But now he was six-feet-four, two hundred and fifty pounds, and while he didn't have that fictional eight-pack, he was in damned good shape considering his professional rugby career had ended five years earlier. Still, he'd been the shortest in his class for years and as skinny as a beanpole. The library had been his happy place, somewhere he could pretend to be strong and tall or a superhero or a Greek god.

And he'd had a crush on Mrs. Phillips, the librarian.

That had all ended, the summer before his junior year which had brought him eight inches and forty pounds. Not his love for literature, but his pathetic crush.

He'd done little over those months except eat, sleep, and groan during the miserable growth spurt. Every bone in his body had hurt, including his toes.

But he'd come out the other side and had picked up rugby.

Which wasn't typical in the States—except Garret had been born in California to an American mother and an Australian father, so he had love for both countries. His parents had divorced when he was in high school, his dad moving back to Australia and Garret's summers permanently spent in a foreign country.

Not that Australia wasn't great. There were parts that were amazing, and he loved the beaches, the people, and rugby. That he'd loved even before his growth spurt. After, he'd gotten good at the sport—so good that he'd managed to play professionally.

The only bad thing about spending summers in Australia had been being away from his friends and missing out on all the high school parties.

His lips curved when he remembered how upset he'd been

about missing Beverly Hawkins' swim party. The girls had skinny dipped, and he hadn't been there to witness it.

God, he'd been such a perv.

Was still a perv.

He was also fucked, he realized the moment that Heather walked into her office. He'd been waiting for the better part of forty-five minutes, her assistant plying him with coffee and snacks, and him assuming that another meeting had run long.

What he *hadn't* expected was for Heather to come in, guns blazing, having already spoken with Katherine—Kay.

How did he know that she'd spoken to Kay?

Probably because she strode across the room, lifted her hand as though to slap him—though she didn't—and glared. "I should slap you," she muttered. "God knows you deserve it. But Kay has this pesky policy against physical violence, and so I'm going to abide by it, as much as it pains me to say."

"I do deserve it," he said.

She indicated he should sit before she crossed behind her desk and sat down herself. "Yes." Her eyes went flinty, steel entering her expression in a way that made this woman way more terrifying than any of his coaches had ever been. "Next time you lie to me, our deal is off the table. I don't fuck around, I don't play games, and I don't force people I work with to date my friends."

"I—"

"Frankly, it was hard fucking enough to get Kay to agree to the date in the first place. She hates meeting new people, and going out in general is like a worst-case scenario for her."

She seemed to be waiting for a response from him, so he told the truth. "Me, too."

Heather threw up her hands, as if she knew he'd say that. "Yes. *Exactly.* Which is why I thought you two would hit it off. She's beautiful and brilliant *and* a homebody." Blue eyes narrowed further. "Like you."

Garret winced. "I—"

"Fucked up."

He nodded. "I was an ass."

"A total ass. A slap-deserving ass." She stood up and started pacing the room. "How dare you call her a cow! Do you know how insulting that is? How fucking dismissive and disgusting?"

"Look"—he pushed to his feet—"Yes, I was an asshole, but I don't need a dressing down from you. I was a prick, case closed, and I already apologized . . . or well, I sent an apology to Kay's apartment this morning."

Heather stared at him long enough that he struggled not to squirm.

"You apologized?" she eventually said.

A nod. "Yes." He sighed. "I shouldn't have said that. It wasn't fair to her or even, women in general. I was showing off for a friend and being a dick. And, not that this matters at all, but I read the book she gave me"—*cough*, hit him with—"last night. It was damned good."

Another long moment of staring and subsequent resisting of squirming.

Why would a grown man feel the urge to squirm in front of a woman half his size?

Because Heather was Heather fucking O'Keith.

And there was just something about her that made people fall in line.

"What happened in chapter twenty-eight?"

"You mean where the hero realized he was an ass and then went to grovel for forgiveness?"

Her lips curved slightly. And it *was* slight, but that barely-there smile was enough to allow Garret to relax.

Marginally.

"I hope you took notes," she said.

"I did. I sent her a gift card to the local bookstore along with a ridiculously expensive notebook and stationary set I picked out myself."

"Hmm."

"And flowers and chocolates and a handwritten note."

Heather crossed to her chair, plunked down into it. "Good. And you're going to ask her out again?"

Garret blinked. "Well, I think I fucked that particular option up, don't you?"

"Hmm." Heather opened a folder on her desk. "Well, it just so happens that I need another man to round out my table at RoboTech's fundraiser this Saturday."

His brows rose, hope bubbled up in his blood. "And will your table include one Kay Hart?"

"Of course, it will." A sage smile. "Now, about your proposal . . ."

CHAPTER FOUR

Kay

FOR THE SECOND time in only a week she was out late, not in bed, and *not* in her sleep pajamas.

Her heels made a little *click click* as she walked into the venue that was housing Heather's fundraising event, and she had to resist the urge to tug at the straps of her bodice. She didn't often wear dresses, and certainly not ones that were so limited in the fabric department.

But after the disastrous date with Garret, she'd wanted to feel sexy.

So, she'd ditched her glasses, put in contacts, and squeezed into her best pushup bra.

Paired with the long navy chiffon gown and she'd pulled her own teen movie makeup montage. The point was that Kay could be glam when she had to—or in this very rare case, when she *wanted* to.

Garret Williams could just stick that up his incredibly yummy ass. Which was so not the point, but still a nice thought.

Who was the cow now?

Hmph. He'd even had the nerve to send her flowers and expect her to accept his apology for being a jerk.

And chocolates, her brain reminded her. *And a gorgeous journal and pen. And*—

"Enough," she growled.

"Are you all right?"

The college-aged boy running the coat check gave her a concerned look, and Kay realized she'd paused in the middle of taking off her jacket and was talking to herself.

Aloud. In public.

Yup. That was absolutely perfect.

Sighing, she forced the frown lines between her brows to relax and curved her lips up into a smile.

"I'm fine." She shoved the coat at him, mentally promised that she'd give him a big tip for being weird later then hurried off with a cheery, "Thank you!"

"Get it together, Hart," she muttered under breath once she was out of earshot. "You'll go in there, say hello, have a bite to eat, a drink, stick around the requisite amount of time, then GTFO."

Feeling better after reminding herself of her plan, Kay lifted her chin and walked through the double doors. Inside, the ballroom had been filled with round tables. They were adorned with gleaming white tablecloths, glittering candles, and gorgeous floral displays.

Each table had a different theme, and the accessories—flowers, vases, and other decorations—had been carefully selected to fit in with that theme.

How did Kay know all of that, just by striding through the door?

Well, the proceeds from tonight's benefit were going to a local literacy charity and because of Kay's experience in publishing, Heather had sicced her assistant Rachel on her. Together they'd selected a different genre of book for each table before going crazy with theming the items.

Kay hadn't minded, however.

The one thing she'd never been able to get enough of was books, and getting to arrange an entire party around the love of her life?

She couldn't lie. It had been the most fun she'd had in ages.

Besides the silent and live auctions, all the centerpieces would be sold. And she had her eye on table ten, which held the historical romance wares. Kay wanted that early edition of Pride and Prejudice, dammit, and she didn't care who she had to take down in the process of getting it.

Heather walked by her then did a double take, jaw falling open.

"Kay?" She stopped, backed up a few feet. "Holy shit. You look amazing! That dress is incredible."

"Thanks—"

Clay, Heather's husband, walked up. "I'm sorry to interrupt, but—Kay?" he exclaimed. "Wow. That's a beautiful color on you."

Kay blushed. That was the reaction she'd wanted from getting dressed up, of course, but she wasn't used to people noticing the way she looked. Still, she was going to take the confidence booster and leave it at that.

Look at her, all mature and shit.

"Go do what you need to do," she told Heather. "I'm going to grab a drink. Are we still sitting together? Or did you bump me for someone more important?"

Heather grinned. "Would I do that to my favorite author?"

"For more donations?" Kay asked. "I would hope so."

"And that"—Heather squeezed her arm—"is why you're a good friend. I'll see you later. Table ten."

Kay waved before heading to the bar.

Once there, she ordered her normal Cosmo before leaning back against the bar top to look around the room. Rachel had worked her magic, turning what could have been a bland ballroom into a really beautiful event. And, though she'd only played a small part in it with the tables, Kay had to admit she was proud of her contribution.

"Here you are," the bartender said.

She turned around, tipped him, and then returned to leaning against the bar, only this time with her Cosmo in hand.

Yeah, she thought as she took a sip, *that was so much better.*

"This must be up your alley."

Kay froze, martini glass at her lips, eyes darting to her left.

She knew that voice.

And the last time she'd heard it, he'd been calling her a cow.

Okay, not exactly the *last time,* but taking a little creative license now and then was kind of her thing.

Garret mirrored her position, leaning against the bar as his eyes trailed down and back up. "You look *incredible,*" he said, lifting a bottle of beer to his lips.

Kay sucked in a breath and nearly choked on her drink. But, hot damn, there was something about a man who drank straight out of a bottle. No fancy glass or prissy cocktail, but a man's man who drank and fucked and—

Apparently, she'd gone too long without writing a true alpha.

Because Garret screamed alpha, especially in that form-fitting suit that showed off his broad shoulders and lean hips and, fuck, but his thighs. There weren't any chicken legs in sight because Garret had *great* thighs.

Kay's mind drifted for a minute, imagined those thighs shoving hers apart as he thrust home. Or maybe her straddling him, riding them both to completion. Or maybe—

She coughed again and then almost choked for a second time when hot, calloused fingers brushed the bare skin of her back.

Had she mentioned that her dress was backless?

A fact that Kay was simultaneously thrilled and dismayed about in that moment.

"Are you okay?" Garret asked, the brush turning into a

gentle pat as she coughed. He snagged her glass from her hand, set it on top of the bar.

She nodded, slowing her breathing as she attempted to not cough up a lung.

"Fine," she eventually managed to rasp. "Thank you."

"Sorry if I startled you." Chocolate eyes met hers. "And I'm sorry for the other night. I was an asshole."

Her lips parted as a surprised breath slipped out.

An apology? No qualifications, no excuses? Just sorry?

Fingertips brushed her spine again. "I didn't want to be there, and I shouldn't have taken it out on you. Further that, what I said was—"

Except, Kay had stopped listening after *I didn't want to be there*.

She'd waited an hour for the man, missed out on her beet salad *and* chocolate soufflé for a jerk who hadn't even wanted to come in the first place.

She'd gotten out of her daytime pajamas for the man.

What. The. Fuck?

The callous fingers on her bare skin lost their appeal, the intimate fantasies speeding through her brain faded away.

"—completely inappropriate and wrong and—"

"I'll have you know—" she started to say before stopping and shaking her head. This man would never get it. "You know what? Never mind. Thanks for the apology. Have a nice life."

She grabbed her glass, started to turn away.

"Wait." He snagged her wrist, causing her cocktail to slosh over the rim of the cup, splashing all along her arm. "Shit." Still holding on to her, he turned for the bar, snagged some napkins from the pile and held them out to her. "Sorry."

"Lot of that going around," she muttered, slipping free of his grip and wiping her arm. She'd need to go to the bathroom to wash it, otherwise she'd be walking around with a sticky hand all night.

Snorting inwardly at that thought—sticky hand, *te-he-he*—

Kay dropped the wad of napkins back onto the bar and lifted her chin. "Goodbye, Garret."

"Wait," he said again, though this time he didn't grab her.

"No, I don't think I will." She whipped around.

He darted around her, stepping right in front of her and forcing her to skid to a stop on her heels. And fuck, because she really didn't want him to, but he smelled amazing.

"I'm fucking this up."

"Ding. Ding. Ding." She took a step to the side and he mimicked the movement. "For God's sake, why won't you leave me alone?"

Garret winced. "Because I'm not normally an asshole."

"Well," she grumbled. "Reiterating the fact you didn't want to go on a date with me at all certainly isn't the way to prove that."

"I—" He sighed. "That's not what I meant."

Kay rolled her eyes. "I mean, I got that loud and clear simply by the fact that you didn't show up."

"I—"

"Then there's the small factor of the bovine reference to my appearance and making fun of my career."

"I—"

"So, yeah, you're not batting that high of an average with the whole *not asshole* thing."

"I read your book."

Kay froze, pulse speeding up.

"I liked it. A lot."

She bit her lip, felt his gaze lock onto the spot, and though she'd written about it in many of her books, imagined it in her author brain plenty of times, Kay had never actually experienced the sensation of a simple look creating such a tangible feeling.

It. Was. Incredible.

She could feel his eyes, could actually *feel* her blood shift, moving toward her lips, plumping them, making them tingle.

Her tongue darted out and his chocolate stare heated, going molten until she could almost sense that melted sweetness dripping down her spine.

He leaned down. Her breath caught.

"I really am sorry."

Just like that, the spell was broken . . . or if not broken exactly, then at least she'd regained a few of her senses.

Kay stepped back and glared at him. Why was he pushing this? Because she didn't believe for one second that he was truly sorry. Sorry he got caught, maybe. Sorry his asshole move might jeopardize—

"Don't worry," she said, clarity finally hitting her brain. "I know that Heather is your investor. I won't do anything to change that."

He waved a hand. "That's not why I'm apologizing. Yes, I'm in business with Heather. Yes, it would be a blow to lose her investment, but this isn't my first rodeo. I'd figure it out."

"Great. Well, kudos to you." She blew out an exasperated breath when she tried to step around him, only to be blocked by him again. "What?" she snapped and poked a finger into his chest. "What's so special about me that you're pushing this?"

He caught her hand, and Kay bit back a gasp at the spark of desire that shot through her at the simple contact. "I—" He shook his head. "I don't know."

And then he was close again. Too close.

Not close enough.

She swallowed hard, heart pounding in the back of her throat, breaths coming in rapid inhalations.

He was going to kiss her.

Oh God. Did she want him to? He was such an ass—

He'd apologized. Seemed to genuinely mean it . . . or at the least was very determined that she believe it.

Garret brushed back a strand of her hair. "I'm not going to say anything," he told her. "Every time I do, I stick my foot in my mouth."

"You're saying something right now."

His lips curved. Her thighs clenched.

Shit. *Shit*. She . . . wanted his mouth to slant across hers.

"You're beautiful." One hand gently cupped her cheek. "And I'm so, *so* sorry."

More words, but she wasn't hearing them because he was coming closer, warm breath on her cheek . . . on her forehead.

He pressed a gentle kiss there before straightening, meeting her no doubt surprised eyes with warm chocolate ones. "I hope someday you'll give me a chance to prove that I'm not usually an ass."

Then he reached behind her, making her breath catch all over again and picked up a glass.

Somehow during all of the apologizing, he'd managed to order her another Cosmo. Her anger eased, not gone completely, but tempered, along with her hurt feelings.

Maybe he wasn't so bad after all.

Carefully, he handed over the drink.

"You didn't drug this, did you?" she blurted.

A raised brow. "Will it get you to accept my apology?"

She shook her head. "Not a chance."

"Damn." Garret smirked. "Not my speed, sweetheart."

She eyed the drink then him.

"I'm happy to pay for a fresh one if you want to watch the bartender mix it up."

Kay bit her lip, watched his eyes heat and drift to that spot again. "No," she said, trying to pretend she wasn't breathless. "That's okay."

One more brush of his fingers, this time along the outside of her arm and making her shiver. "I'll see you later."

And then he was gone, taking the rest of her anger along with him.

Maybe she was a pushover who forgave too easily.

But . . . maybe she wasn't.

CHAPTER FIVE

Garret

HE SAW the moment Kay clued into the fact that they would be sitting next to each other at dinner.

Consternation rolled across her expression, followed by softness and then maybe irritation. She was almost an open book with those feelings written on her face, and he had the feeling that if he got to know her better, he'd be able to read them as easily as one of her books.

And he *wanted* to know her better.

Whether or not she believed it, since that night he'd thought of little else aside finding a way to win her over, to prove that he wasn't always a jerk, and to convince her to give him a second chance for a first date.

Garret pulled Kay's chair out for her and waited for her to sit, feeling as though he were playing an intense game of chicken.

Would she cave and sit?

Or would he be relegated to the reject table?

Heather was on Kay's other side. "Sit, please, everyone." Kay, next to him, released a barely audible sigh, but did sit.

Heather glanced back at him and winked.

Garret plunked down into his chair, lest Kay change her mind about relegating him to the rejects.

"Did you like the journal?" he asked, not wanting to remind her of their disastrous first date any more than necessary, but also more than a little desperate to see if he'd picked correctly.

Her expression gentled, and he sent up a prayer that he might have actually chosen something right to say for a change.

"Yes, I did," she said. "It was absolutely lovely."

He shrugged. "The least I could do."

She dropped her chin to her chest, sighed, and Garret's stomach clenched. *Shit.* What had he done now?

And, *fuck it all*, but why did he care so much?

"Can we just start over?" she asked.

If he'd been hit over the head with a two-by-four, Garret wouldn't have been more shocked. "Do you . . . do you *want* to?"

She glanced up at him from beneath her lashes, smiled shyly. "Yes."

His heart skipped a beat, and he realized he was in the best type of trouble. The kind that led to monogamy and picket fences and, yes, it was way too fucking soon to even be considering that in the slightest . . . but—

There was something different about this woman.

Something he knew he wanted to explore further.

"Okay."

Her smile widened. "Okay."

The servers were coming around with salads and so Garret waited for their plates to be delivered. "Why writing?" he asked once the waiter had retreated.

Kay bit her lip again and that little flash of white against pink, the glistening of soft skin from the moisture left behind, the desire for it to be *his* teeth all contributed to making his cock twitch.

He hadn't touched her, and he was at risk of embarrassing himself.

"I was super shy as a kid," she said and shrugged. "Stories gave me a way to get all my words out and onto a page without worrying if I was going to stutter or screw up or miss something." She reached into her purse and pulled out a tiny notebook, along with a pencil and an eraser shaped like a fox. "My weapons!" she joked. "The best part was that this one"—she made the little fox run across the tablecloth—"has magical erasing powers."

"A marvelous feat of engineering."

She smiled up at him. "Exactly." Then shyness seemed to take over because her gaze drifted down. She seemed to realize her plate was still full and took a bite of salad.

He did the same.

"So," she said a few moments later, "why rugby?"

Garret shrugged. "I loved watching it growing up. My dad's Australian, and it's obviously much more popular there. When my parents split up, I'd go there and visit my dad, and I sort of fell into it."

One half of her mouth turned up. "Fell into it so well you were good enough to play professionally."

"I got lucky, and I definitely was never the best guy on the team." He speared some lettuce with his fork. "Do you know anything about rugby?"

Amusement played across her gorgeous face. "I know I like rugby romance."

He tilted his head to the side. "That's a thing?"

"Oh yeah, it's a thing."

"Well, damn."

She grinned, pointed at his plate "Eat your salad before your jaw falls off."

He snorted but shoved the bite hanging off his fork into his mouth, chewed and swallowed. "Where'd you grow up?"

They exchanged first date pleasantries, finding out that

they'd both grown up in California, though Kay was born and raised in the Bay Area, while Garret had been in L.A. until his rugby career had taken off. He'd moved back to the States and up to Northern California just a few months before.

"Did you learn to surf?" she asked, after they'd both discovered they were only children.

Garret shuddered. "No. The guys tried, but I'm hopeless."

Kay smiled. "I learned. The water was freezing, and I was freaked out the whole time that a Great White was going to attack me, but I managed to get up on a couple of waves at least."

"Nice." He raised his fist for her to bump, and their eyes met when even that tiny bit of contact made his nerves spark.

"Why does that keep happening?" she breathed.

"I don't know." A beat. "But I don't hate it."

Her laughter made his heart skip a beat—something that was starting to become a regular occurrence with this woman.

They talked about her books during the main course, laughed over a few of Garret's rugby stories during dessert—an American rookie had led to no small amount of good-natured teasing and pranks. She had him in absolute stitches as she relayed a tale about how she'd been so mad at a former boyfriend that she'd made him the impotent villain in an early book as the live auction was going on.

He clamped a hand over his mouth, nudged her with his shoulder. "You almost made me buy that trip to Maui," he said with a mock-glare.

"I'd make you take me," she teased.

He bent close. "Should I be worried you're going to make *me* impotent in a future book?"

She leaned in conspiratorially. "I *was* going to kill you off."

"What about now?" He turned, and suddenly their lips very close together.

"I'm considering my options."

"I—"

Applause broke out around them and Garret blinked, trying to sort out the reason until he realized the first portion of the live auction was over.

Kay stood. "I'm going to hit the ladies room before they start bidding on these babies." Her fingers traced over the centerpiece of books in the middle of the table. "I've had my eye on this one since I first gave Rachel the idea for them."

He rose as well. "Do you want me to get you another drink? I promise I won't spill this one on you."

Her smile lit up her face, and Garret knew in that moment that he'd do anything for this woman. "That would be great. Thank you." And with a quick word to Heather—asking her to watch her purse—and a soft touch to the spine of one book in particular, a whispered, "I'll be back for you," she hurried across the room.

Heather glanced up at him, raised her brows.

"I'm an idiot, and you know all."

Clay's mouth quirked. "Words my wife loves to hear."

"She's amazing."

"Of course, she is," Heather said. "She's *my* friend."

CHAPTER SIX

Kay

SHE WAS TRAPPED in the bathroom.

Kay was literally trapped in the bathroom, and her Jane Austen book was in danger.

Why had she decided to pee?

Or more importantly, why had she decided to leave her purse and, inside of it her cell phone, with Heather?

Oh yeah, because she hadn't wanted to wrestle with her full-length dress and heels *and* a purse all while trying to hover so her butt didn't touch a gross public toilet seat.

"Hello?" she said again, trying the door handle for the umpteenth time.

It still didn't budge, and she'd lost count of how many times she'd knocked on the door, trying to get someone's attention. All she knew was that she'd been locked in the room for what seemed to be an inordinate amount of time.

"Hello?"

Why did the stalls have to be floor to ceiling with actual doors?

What she wouldn't give in that moment to be able to crawl

out beneath that shin-high gap most public bathrooms sported, dirty, germ-filled floor aside.

Who cared? Her Austen was *in danger.*

"It's going to be fine," she murmured. They were auctioning the tables from one upward. Her Austen was number ten.

She had plenty of time.

Except . . . how long had she been trapped?

"Shit!" she muttered then raised her voice. "Help!" she called. "*Help!*"

Finally, she heard footsteps. "Hello?"

"Hello?" she said. "I'm stuck in the stall."

"Oh no," came a female voice. "This one?" The handle jiggled from the outside.

"Yes."

"Okay, let me try." It wiggled some more. "Can you turn it at all?"

Kay and her mystery female help worked for a few minutes more, trying to get the handle to move or the lock to disengage, all to no avail.

"Shoot," the woman eventually said. "I can't get it to budge. I'm going to see if I can find an employee. Maybe they have a key or a screwdriver or something."

"Thank you so much," Kay said, even though her heart was sinking as the minutes passed. There was no way the auctioneer wasn't getting close to her table, and the likelihood of that early edition of *Pride and Prejudice* being added to her collection was dropping with each passing moment.

A few minutes passed, and the woman reappeared . . . or at least her voice did. "I found an employee, and they called maintenance, but are you by any chance Kay?"

"Yes," she said. "Why?"

"Because there's a guy out here named Garret. I guess he got worried and came looking."

"Oh."

That was sweet.

"He says he can try to fix the handle if you're comfortable."

"I'm comfortable with anything that gets me out of this stall."

"I had a feeling," the woman said. "Let me grab him."

A few moments later, Kay heard quick footsteps across the tile floor. "Sweetheart? Which stall are you in?"

Her pulse jumped at the endearment—too soon and yet she liked the way it made her feel. As though she were special to him. "I'm here," she said, knocking on the door.

"Okay, I'm going to try . . ." And he spent a few minutes repeating the process Kay had tried by herself and also with her female helper, without success. "Damn," he muttered. "You're really stuck. Let me see if there's any progress on the maintenance guy. You okay in there for a few more minutes?"

It wasn't like she had a choice, but Kay bit back an annoyed reply. Garret was trying to help, and getting snappy wouldn't help.

The Austen would be there when she got out, or it wouldn't.

That was just the way it was going to be.

Garret came back into the bathroom, relaying he'd been told it would only be a few more minutes before they came, but when a solid fifteen minutes passed, he ordered her to stand back.

And with a grunt and hard shove of his shoulder, he broke the lock, slamming the door into the stall. It crashed against the wall with surprising force, and the half of her that was impressed with his strength was really glad she'd been standing well out of the way.

The other half of her launched herself over the splinters of wood and into his arms.

"Thank you!" she exclaimed, squeezing him tightly. "Thank you so much." She stepped out of his arms, turned to the petite blonde standing in the doorway. "And thank *you* for not leaving me. I was really worried there for a minute."

"I'm Claire," the woman said. "And I glad you were rescued."

"Kay." She laughed. "But I guess you knew that already. Thank you again."

Claire left as Kay spun back to face Garret. "I've got to see if I can get back for the table auction. My Austen—"

Her gut clenched.

Because his expression said it all.

"It's gone?"

He nodded. "I'm sorry. I heard the bids close on it when I went to find the maintenance guy."

"Oh." She sucked in a breath and pushed down her disappointment. It was only a book. There would be others. "Did it go for a lot?"

"Over two thousand."

Kay's eyes widened. "Really? Well, at least they got their money's worth."

"Yeah." He took her hand. "Do you want to go back to the party?"

"Not really."

"Okay." Garret tucked her palm into the crook of his arm. "I'll walk you to your car."

"I took an Uber."

His lips twitched. "I'm grasping at straws here. So, should I call you an Uber or do you want a ride home?"

Kay shook off her disappointment. "Sorry," she said. "I'm just a mixture of bummed about the book and shook up from being trapped in a bathroom stall for . . ." She paused. "How long exactly?"

"Close to an hour."

"Shit."

He snorted. "Literally."

"Garret!" But then she was laughing, too, and by the time they both stopped, she felt better. "Thanks," she said. Her hand still rested on his forearm, and she gave the hard muscle a squeeze.

"You're welcome."

"Did you bring a coat?"

"Yes," she said. "I just need to get the ticket out of my—" She smacked her forehead. "My purse! I'm an idiot. I forgot I left it with—"

Garret held it up.

"She got pulled away from the table. I promised to keep it safe." He pretended to model it for a few seconds and had her in hysterics. "I think it goes with my outfit, don't you?"

She patted his arm. "Only a truly secure man would say that."

"You know it." He handed her the purse then steered them toward coat check. "Let's grab your jacket, and I'll drive you home."

"That sounds great."

———

HER COAT FELT a little heavy when she put it on, but she attributed it to exhaustion from her crazy evening. First Garret, then the bathroom, and now the multitude of sparks flying as he drove her home.

He held her hand, stroking little circles on the back of her wrist as they drove. Bolts of pleasure shot up her arm and then down. Straight down between her thighs.

Yup, she was getting hot from a simple caress.

Thus was the power of Garret Williams.

He regaled her with a few more tales but didn't take over the conversation. For as much as he spoke, he seemed to make sure she talked twice as much, and his questions were interesting and fun, ranging from thoughtful to simple small talk.

She'd answered everything from "Where do you come up

with your character names?" to "What's your favorite thing to binge right now?" to "What did your parents do growing up?"

Her answers had been: she had a master list of character names she added to every time she heard a good name, *Killing Eve*, and school teachers, respectively.

"Star Wars or Star Trek?"

She slanted her eyes at him, felt her lips twitch and then they both said, "Star Wars" at the same time.

He laughed, brushed his fingers along her wrist again, and her breath caught.

Garret was . . . well, he was being the perfect date.

Of course, he was also spinning a web around her, drawing her in, tugging her close—

Or maybe that just what her body wanted.

Or her brain.

Shh, her mind said. *Don't ruin this for us.*

Apparently, all of her wanted Garret and she couldn't just chalk it up to hormones. Nope. He was smart and funny and kind, and the hug after he'd rescued her from the bathroom hadn't been nearly enough contact.

Damn Heather for her matchmaking skills. If she liked Garret and went out with him then she'd never hear the end of it—

And now Kay was grasping at straws to distance herself.

Because she was scared.

Because she really liked him.

Ugh.

"Take a right at the signal," she said softly.

As though sensing she was going around in circles in her mind, Garret just nodded and then silently followed the rest of her directions until he was pulling into her driveway. She owned a house south of the City and though it was ridiculously small—she mentally shook her fist at the price of Bay Area real estate—Kay was very proud of it. The little Craftsman had a wide front porch that was dotted with pots of hardy flowers she'd somehow managed to keep alive.

And considering her black thumb, *that* was saying something.

"Thanks," she said softly and then bit her lip, unsure what to say and suddenly nervous.

"This place is great," he said, staring at her house. "Is it blue or gray? It's hard to tell in this light."

Her lips curved, and she relaxed. "It's blue-gray. Do you"—she sucked in a breath—"do you want to come in?"

There.

That might have been the bravest thing she'd ever done with a man. Inviting him into her house and not even under the guise of a nightcap. She wasn't necessarily the type of girl to sleep with someone after a date or two, however good or bad they were. But with Garret, she thought she *could* be.

Quiet filled the car, and Kay felt her cheeks heat.

Chocolate eyes locked onto hers, desire in their depths, and yet he didn't move to get out of the car.

His expression went rueful. "I *want* to come in, but I'm not going to. I consider myself on probation after our first date."

"Probation?" she asked, head tilting to study him. A mix of relief and disappointment coursed through her, which told her he was probably right in his decision to not come in. Yes, she wanted him, but yes, there was also a part of her waiting for the asshole to reappear.

It was just too soon.

He cupped her cheek. "You need time to get to know me." One half of his mouth curved. "The not jerky version."

"How long do you propose this probationary period to last?"

"Hmm. Three months should do it?"

Her heart jumped. *Three months?* He was considering—

Fingers on her wrist again. "Will you go out with me sometime next week?"

"I'd like that." She reached into her purse and handed him her card. "Here's my email."

"No phone number?"

She shook her head, reached for the handle. "We'll work up to it."

A grin that made her thighs clench. "I'm good with working up to things. But"—his eyes scorched her—"I'd like to kiss you goodnight."

Her mouth went dry, longing pulsed through her.

But then his expression transformed, going all innocent as he shrugged. "I mean, if you want to. No big deal."

Amusement filled her. "Nope. No can do, bucko," she told him. "You're on probation, remember?" Disappointment crossed his gorgeous face, and Kay bit back a smile. "But . . . I can kiss you because *I'm* not the one aboard the paddy wagon."

One brow rose. "Paddy wagon?"

She leaned across the consul. "Shut up."

She kissed him.

From the moment her lips touched his, all was right in the world. His mouth had been slack with surprise, but he quickly recovered, sliding his hands into her hair, tugging her close, angling her head so they fit perfectly together. Kay might have been the one to initiate the kiss, but Garret was the one to own it.

To own *her*.

His tongue slipped inside, tangling with hers. Heat and moisture and . . . *fuck* but he could kiss good.

Not proper English in the slightest, and her editor would be appalled at her grammar. But as his hands trailed down her spine and his tongue slid in and out of her mouth in a rhythm that had her seeing stars, all she could think was—

Good.

More.

Naked.

Now.

And that was the moment Garret pulled back. He pushed out his door, walked around the front of his car, and opened hers.

He extended a hand, and her desire-addled brain had Kay trailing him mutely to the house. "Keys?" he asked once they'd stopped on the porch.

She blinked, pulled them out of her purse.

Garret snagged them from her, unlocked the door. Then he kissed her one more time, slipping a hand underneath her coat, wrapping it around her waist, and pulling her flush against him. His chest hard and his cock . . . well, *that* was hard, too. She arched, aching to be closer, for the thin layers of her dress and his clothes to disappear.

His hand slid a little lower, fingertips teasing the top of her ass, before he pulled back with a curse. "You'll be the death of me, sweetheart." And though he was breathing hard, his eyes danced. "Dangerous kisses. Assaulting me with paperbacks—"

Kay felt her cheeks go red. "I'll have you know, I'm not normally prone to violence."

A kiss to her forehead as he opened the door.

"I certainly deserved more than the potential risk of a paper cut."

He nudged her inside.

"It's ok—"

"Three months," he said softly and nudged her inside before closing the door, leaving them separated by the planks of wood. "Lock up." His voice was muffled.

She reached for the handle. "Garret—"

"*Lock up.*"

Kay sighed loud enough for him to hear, but her lips were curved.

She locked the door, pulled out her phone, scrolled down to Heather's number, and shot off a quick text.

"Garret?" she called as she waited.

"Yes?"

Buzz. Buzz.

Her fingers moved furiously across the keyboard . . . and *send.*

"Kay?"

"There's my number," she said.

"What—" He broke off, no doubt felt the buzz of the text she sent him "*Oh.*"

"Consider it supervised release."

He laughed, a loud guffaw that resounded through the door and warmed her heart.

"Goodnight, Garret."

"Goodnight, sweetheart."

She heard his footsteps as he crossed the porch and made his way down the steps. Then listened to the slam of the car door and the rev of the engine as it started up. Kay was just starting to shrug out of her coat when her cell buzzed.

Look in your right coat pocket.

"What?"

Her hand darted down, felt something hard and rectangular and—

She pulled out a book.

The book.

She opened it, surprised when a note fell out. Scooping it up from the floor, she unfolded it and read:

Sorry I was late rescuing you. I had something really impor-
tant I needed to bid on. Heather promised the other books
would be delivered next week sometime. I figured you would
want to keep this one safe.
-G

When had he found time to write her a note?

But then she smiled, remembered Garret talking to the kid at the coat check stand. He'd been there awhile, longer than it should have taken to just pick up her jacket.

Sneaky man.

Wonderful man.

She held the book to her chest as she typed out a text.

Thank you. So, so much. Then before he could reply, she added, *I think you should be up to unsupervised release now.*

His response made her laugh aloud.

Two months and twenty-nine days.

CHAPTER SEVEN

Garret, Two months and twenty-eight days later

HE WHISTLED as he hopped up the stairs leading to Kay's house then softly knocked on the front door.

They'd fallen into a pleasant routine over the last few months. During the week, he'd pop over after work and they'd eat dinner together. On the weekends, they would hang out, walk around the city, go to the beach or see a movie. It was funny—in a crazy-because-it-felt-so-right-way rather than a funny-but-weird way—but since the night of the fundraiser they hadn't gone a day without seeing each other.

Garret liked that. A lot.

In fact, he loved it.

He loved *her*.

When his quiet knock wasn't answered—Garret used his key to let himself in. They'd learned a lot about each other over the last months, and one of the first things he'd needed to grasp —or risk the wrath of his woman—was that if Kay was writing she didn't like to be interrupted.

Typically, she'd be waiting for him when he got there, snuggled up in cute pajamas and a glass of wine in her hand as she answered the door.

But if she didn't answer the knock, that meant the muse was still talking and it was better for everyone—and most especially *him*—if he didn't interrupt Kay while she was working.

His first—and only—interruption hadn't been intentional. In fact, he'd been worried when she hadn't answered her door or her phone. Finally, after multiple rings of the bell, she'd pounded down the stairs, whipped open the door, and he'd learned the hard way to not interrupt the Beast—his teasing nickname for her author persona—at work. No way did he want to endure another round of glaring and grumbling.

She'd apologized later for being grumpy, and he'd teased her by threatening to put *her* on probation. But Garret got it. A jarring intrusion while working on something important was bound to make anyone cranky.

Smiling, he silently let himself into the house, closing and locking the door behind him.

He'd wait thirty minutes then order a pizza.

It hadn't taken him long to understand that the smell of pepperoni tended to lure Kay out of her writing cave.

Plan in mind, he was mentally patting himself on his back as he turned for the living room.

Only to stop halfway, his jaw falling open.

Kay stood on the bottom step, wearing only a pair of under-wear and bra.

Lacy underwear.

A see-through bra.

His cock hardened, his pulse jumped, and he didn't think, just strode over, wrapped his arms around her waist, and lifted her up. Her mouth found his, tongues meeting, twining together, dancing in a pattern they'd perfected over the last months.

But this? Kay nearly naked in his arms?

They hadn't perfected *this*.

Probation wasn't up for another day.

Yes, he'd been counting.

Kay broke away, gasping for air as he kissed his way down her neck, trailed his mouth across her collarbone, nipped the top of one breast. She gasped, wound her hands into his hair to hold him in place and so he repeated the action, soothing it with a flick of his tongue before moving to her other breast.

Then somehow her bra disappeared—or rather, his mind hazed over the specific details of the undressing because suddenly, he had a gorgeous pair of breasts in front of him that he *needed* to get his mouth on.

"Yes," Kay said, tugging him toward one nipple. "Please, Garret. Oh *God. Yes.*"

He switched sides as her hands reached for the button on his slacks, fumbling with the little circle until it slipped free and she was able to reach inside his boxer briefs to grip him.

Stars flashed behind his lids, his hips thrust forward, and he groaned.

He'd been imagining this for three long months, planning all the things he was going to do to make the night incredible and perfect and unforgettable for his woman. Yes, they'd touched each other, engaged in some seriously heavy petting, but it had all been through clothes. Garret had insisted on it, despite her pleas, despite his near perpetual blue balls, because he'd promised himself that he wouldn't sleep with Kay until she trusted him completely, whether that took three months or three years.

They'd spent many nights together, but he hadn't slept over.

They'd touched, but not skin to skin.

They'd kissed, but only from the throat up.

But last week, he'd finally seen it.

Kay's last wall had fallen, the final bit of distance she'd kept between them had disappeared, and Garret knew his patience—and hers—had all been worth it.

He trusted her like he'd never trusted another person. She

knew everything about him, good and bad and in between, and . . . he loved her, more than he'd thought possible to love another person.

She was his heart. It was as simple as that.

And, as usual, this beautiful, wonderful, kind woman had surprised him.

This time it wasn't assault by novel or confronting him in a restaurant or getting locked in a bathroom stall.

Instead, she'd decided she'd had enough and was going after what she wanted.

"Garret?" she asked, stroking him and making every single one of his carefully laid out plans poof right out of his head.

"Yeah?" he gritted out, clambering for control and not finding it.

"Can we"—another stroke that had him groaning—"skip the foreplay. Just this once?"

His eyes shot to hers.

She shrugged. "We've kinda had three months of foreplay already."

Good point. *Excellent* point.

Garret nodded. "You're right." He swept her up into his arms, pounded up the stairs. He was inside her bedroom seconds later, tossing Kay onto the mattress, tearing off his clothes.

She slipped out of her panties, tossed them aside. Breathtakingly naked, Kay reached for a packet from her nightstand. "Catch." She lobbed it at him.

Gotta love a woman with a plan.

Garret caught the condom, tore it open, and rolled it on. He was on top of her by the next second, spreading her thighs, kneeling in between, and then . . . his heart had him pausing.

"You sure?" he asked.

Her eyes softened and she reached up to cup his jaw. "I'm sure."

"Good," he said and thrust inside. "Because I'm keeping

you." Her eyes had flitted closed as he'd pushed home, lips parting on a moan, but at his words she peeled back her lids.

Warmth. This woman just imparted so much fucking warmth.

He looked at her and felt . . . everything.

Possessiveness, desire, heat . . . *love.*

She made him want to write sonnets and horrible love songs, to shout her name from rooftops.

"I love you," he said.

Her hand came up to rest on his chest, just over his heart. "I love you, too," she said, tears making the pretty brown of her irises glitter.

They stared at each other for a long moment. Then Kay shifted beneath him, hips undulating and sucking every rational thought from his mind. "I know I'm supposed to be the romance writer here, and I should be appreciating you and the loveliness of this moment, but can we appreciate it later?" She shifted again. "Because I *really* need you to move."

"Yeah?" He pulled out, slid back in.

She nodded. "Fuck now. Romance later."

Another thrust. Another shared moan.

"Words to live by?" he managed to ask.

"I'd rather live with you," she said.

"Me too, sweetheart, me too."

Then they weren't talking, or at least they didn't have any more room in their brains for talking. The moment became about sensation—for nerves to fire, for caresses and soft touches to leave goosebumps in their wake, for pleasure to build, orgasms to pull them each over into the abyss, and . . . for hearts to feel.

After, as they lay together, bodies intertwined, Garret knew *his* heart wouldn't ever belong to another.

Kay owned it.

And that was perfectly fine with him.

BAD TEXT

CHAPTER 1

Lorelai

Buzz. Buzz.

Lori groaned and rolled over, scrambling for her cell and hitting the side button to shut it up. Then she burrowed her head into her pillow and tried to go back to sleep.

Her eyes slid closed. Her breathing slowed—

Buzz. Buzz.

"Ugh," she muttered, scrabbling for her phone again. Her fingers closed around the case, bringing it up to her face, and glancing at the too-bright screen with scrunched up eyes.

Fuck, that was intense.

Buzz. Buzz.

Squinting, she looked at the home screen, saw a trail of three texts.

Hey, baby, the first one read. *I'm so glad I met you tonight.*

I hope that you really DO want this, the second one said.

The third one . . . was a picture.

Call it stupidity, or perhaps it was just because she'd been woken up in the middle of the night and her brain was mush, but for whatever reason, Lori touched the text bubble with the picture.

A second later, the screen unlocked.

And then—

"Um . . ." She blinked, looked again. "Um. *Wow.*"

There on the screen was . . . holy balls—no pun intended—but there were . . . well, *balls* and a penis and abs and—

Look, she'd seen her fair share of dick pics, being a single woman in her early thirties. They seemed to appear in her inbox in uninvited droves and while this one was definitely *not* invited, it was also . . . kind of the best she'd ever seen.

Her phone buzzed again, and she glanced at the screen.

You there?

Lori froze, eyes glued to the picture and knowing she had a choice to make. One to pretend to be whoever *you* was in order to obtain more photos. Gross, but it had been a long time since she'd . . . fine, here was her inner perv talking, seen a penis in the flesh.

Ick. Not the best thought.

But it was two in the morning, she'd been an idiot to not have her phone on Do Not Disturb, and . . . it had been A. Really. Long. Time.

However, even being pent-up sexually, she still had enough of a moral center that she felt the need to respond to the man and tell him he had the wrong number.

But maybe if she waited long enough, she might get another pic?

Just one to look at—briefly—before she'd promptly delete it and—

Her eyes drifted back down to her phone, to the words this

time, and her pesky conscience reared its head. Sighing, she let her fingers work on the keyboard.

You have the wrong number.

Silence.
Several long minutes of silence.
Then,

Oh, fuck. I'm so sorry.

She couldn't help it—she laughed, but sent back,

It's . . . not okay, I guess. But don't worry. I'll delete it and we can pretend it never happened.

A beat.

Thank you. And again, I'm so sorry.

Which was the point she couldn't help herself from replying with,

Next you send a dick pic, leave off your head.

Lori winced.

*The head attached to your neck, not the one on your . . . well . . . . *finger pointing down emoji**

There was no response for a long time. But eventually her cell vibrated again and—

Noted.

Sighing and sending out sad, pathetic thoughts to the universe for having to be a good person and noting that she'd better get some good karma for being nice about an unsolicited dick pic in the middle of the night, she deleted the photo. Then sent a screen shot of their chain—sans pic—as proof to the mysterious, albeit gorgeous man with the yummiest cock she'd ever laid eyes on that she had, in fact, deleted the photo.

A buzz.

Thanks.

She wrinkled her nose and flopped onto her back, wide awake and huffy about it. Then made huffier when her phone vibrated again.

Um. Does that thing happen a lot?

Me receiving unwanted photos of penises? Or the man sending them apologizing?

Either. Both.

She grinned.

Yes to the first. No to the second.

Fuck. Men are assholes.

At least the latest one had a pretty face.

And a pretty something else, but that was beside the point. Lori set her cell on the bedside table again and started to lie back.

Buzz. Buzz.

"Oh my fucking God," she muttered and scooped up her phone, glaring at the screen as she read.

Then her lips twitched.

How about you send me your pretty face?

The man either had the slickest game on the planet or he was seriously horrible at reading the opposite sex.

That's a no.

Though, she was the one who kept engaging, so what did that make her? Rolling her eyes, she turned on Do Not Disturb, placed her cell on the bedside table—for the *final* time—and then cuddled back under the blankets. She had to get up in four hours. She was going to sleep, and that would happen *right* now.

Right. Now.

Right—

Fuck it, she was going to look.

Flipping to her side, she reached for her phone, tilting it up just enough to see the screen. A response was there. Of course, it was. But nope. She was not opening it. No way. No how. No—

Oh, look. Her Face ID magically unlocked the screen and loaded her messages.

Please?

She snorted.

Nope.

Pretty please with sugar on top?

What are you? Five?

I'm thirty-five, actually. And totally helpless when it comes to women.

I can see that.

Ouch.

A beat before he sent,

So now will you show me your face?

She shook her head. This man was persistent, if nothing else.

Going into the creepy territory, Mr. Thirty-Five.

Victory!

thinking emoji

I'm no longer helpless. I'm creepy.

Lori couldn't help it. She outright laughed. Oh boy, this man was something else.

You do realize it's almost three in the morning, right?

You're the one responding to my messages.

You're the one who sent the filthy dick pic in the first place.

She asked for it!

Her lips curved. Now, *this* was a story she had to hear. Lori sat up, tucking her fuzzy purple comforter under her arms as she went. A moment later, she'd fluffed the pillows up behind her back and then flicked on the light. Only once she was comfortable did she send a reply.

How exactly did she "ask for it?"

The little ". . ." bubble appeared at the bottom of the screen. Then disappeared. Then reappeared and stayed there for a while. The reply that buzzed into her cell made her understand why it took a while. He'd sent a dissertation.

Well, there was this girl in the bar. Hannah. Okay, I'm not the type of person to go to bars usually, but I'm new in town and jet-lagged and I figured it was better than just staying in my condo staring at the empty walls since only half of my furniture arrived and none of that arrived furniture included my TV. Also, I have no internet because they're coming tomorrow.

There was a pause here where she assumed he was waiting for her to respond and so she did.

Tell me more.

More bubbles appearing and disappearing until her cell vibrated.

So I went out looking for a diner or coffee shop or whatever, but the only place that was open was a bar—

She snorted. Sure, it was.

I had a couple of drinks—

Another snort. A couple, right.

Next thing I know, Hannah came over and we spent a few

hours eating, drinking, and talking but then she had to go. Before she left, though, she wrote her number on my hand—

How very high school.

—and told me to text her something she could use to relax her later—and here, she patted my crotch—

Wow.

I mean, who does that? She could have just put the number in my phone. Anyway, by the time my drunk ass got over the feel of her hand on my cock and I'd really processed what she'd done, she was gone, and I was paying a big bill.

She pressed her lips together.

You seem awfully sober now.

A beat then,

Being the type of asshole to send an unsolicited dick pic will do that to a man.

She snorted.

I'm not sure that's true.

Well, true or not, I obviously got played.

Lori considered all that then sent,

Pictures, or it isn't true.

There was a long silence before she got a reply.

Um, isn't that what got us into this problem in the first place?

She grinned.

I meant of the number this Hannah wrote on your hand.

Oh.

A few seconds later, her cell buzzed, and another pic appeared on her screen. This one was also naked, but because it was a picture of a naked palm, it was less exciting. Though those thick fingers, yo. And . . . she was an idiot, but it was now after three in the morning, she was texting a stranger, and so she was allowed to be a bit delirious. Shaking her head, she focused on the photo.

Sure enough, there was a scrawling phone number on his skin.

Except—

That's not a 1.

What?

At the end. That's a 7.

Lori's stomach was clenching tighter than during her Pilates class. Okay, bad analogy, but the point was that she was trying not to laugh. Trying didn't mean she succeeded. In fact, she failed miserably and missed the next three texts her mystery man had sent.

That's a 1.

Oh my fucking God, that's NOT a 1.

Kill me. Now.

By the time she could breathe again, or at least by the time her laughter had been reduced to giggles, several minutes had passed.

Then her phone buzzed again.

It's a 7.

Lori grinned, almost able to hear the defeat in his tone, even though all she had was words on a screen. But this man, whoever he was, had personality.

I'm going to go throw myself off a bridge.

She paused, concern now mixing with amusement.

Is this joking or are you actually suicidal? Because, in the grand scheme of things, a dick pic isn't the end of the world. I'm not emotionally scarred and plus, I deleted it.

A beat, then,

Too bad you can't delete my unending shame.

But seriously, I'm sorry . . . about everything. The picture. The comments — that was insensitive. I'm not that kind of guy.

Hmm. Well, *that* was interesting.

Why type of guy are you?

No reply. For a solid three minutes. For long enough that Lori realized she'd clearly pushed the wrong button and no matter how pretty his dick or how interesting his text personality was, they were done. An hour of texting and strangely, she found that disappointing.

Sighing, she plugged her cell back in.

Well, another one driven away. Somehow that wasn't surprising in the least. Too bad this time she hadn't even known his name.

Her eyes slid closed, sleep finally welled up and surrounded her, and she fell head-long into darkness.

And missed the final *buzz-buzz* from the mystery man.

Missed him saying,

I'm . . . I don't know who I am.

CHAPTER 2

Lorelai

OH GOD, she was late.

Late.

Normally, that wouldn't matter. Her boss, Heather O'Keith didn't really care what hours her engineers kept, so long as the deadlines were met. The trouble was that today she had a meeting.

With her boss.

A meeting she was going to be late for.

"Shit," she muttered, shrugging on her backpack and snatching her phone from the charger. She'd somehow turned down the volume on her cell and hadn't heard the alarm until it had been going off for forty-five minutes.

That was why she didn't stay up all night anymore.

Her sleep-hangover was deadly when it came to hearing alarm clocks.

"Fuck," she hissed, stubbing a toe and hopping around on one foot for a few moments before throwing on her "fancy" sneakers. Sneakers, since no one in her department dressed in anything more formal than jeans, tennis shoes, and a tee, but nice because she still had a meeting with her boss.

Classy, she was.

Okay, so backpack, check. Phone, check. Jacket, check. Clothes on all pertinent portions of her body because she really didn't want to live her nightmare of showing up at work pants-less, check. Coffee . . . she wanted. Badly. But she would have to wait.

Ugh.

Regardless of her inner, ugh-ing, Lori hurried to her front door and fumbled through it in her daily struggle of heavy wooden panel meets a bulky jacket and a giant backpack with a phone in one hand.

It wasn't pretty.

Ever.

And also why she didn't realize that her new neighbor was standing in the hall, thoroughly entertained by the process until a hand landed on the door above her head, stopping it from swinging closed on her leg.

"Thank—"

She glanced up and *every single muscle* in her body locked in place. It was—

She shook her head, tried to clear it, because it couldn't possibly be . . .

No. No fucking way.

Warm fingers wrapped around her arm, tugging her gently forward so the door could shut. Absently, Lori checked the knob to make sure it had locked.

She reached for the fingers on her arm, not necessarily to push him away, but to flip over his palm and see—

"Are you okay?"

Hot sunshine burning into her skin, drifting down her spine, slipping between her legs. Her pussy clenched . . . because she knew *exactly* what this guy was packing.

"What's your name?" she whispered.

A pause then, "Logan."

"Are you still jet-lagged?"

"Um. Yes?" He stepped back, head tilting and drawing her focus to deep brown eyes and sun-kissed olive skin. If he'd told her the reason he was jet-lagged was because he had just stepped off a yacht in the Mediterranean then Lori would have absolutely believed it.

"It's not a 1," she murmured.

And waited.

Luckily, it didn't take long.

His eyes went wide, and he took another step back, gaze flicking from her apartment door to her neighbor's—or well, now *his* apartment door.

"When did you move in?" she asked.

Logan blinked, focused back on her. "Yesterday."

"Cool," she said, suddenly realizing that she should be feeling awkward because she'd seen this man's business parts and not focusing on how much her body was telling her that it had been a really *long* time since she'd seen said business end of a man. Oh, and that there wasn't any time like the present to remedy that fact, might not be the best strategy moving forward.

But he has a great cock—

Focus.

Great. Now she was mentally arguing with herself.

That was the surest sign of sanity. Totally.

She turned to leave.

He snagged her arm. "What's your name?"

Figuring she owed him that much based solely on the fact they were neighbors but also reinforced by the fact that she'd seen his penis, she said, "Lorelai. But mostly everyone calls me Lori."

"Lori," he murmured.

Her phone buzzed, and she glanced down at the reminder

that she had five minutes to make it to her meeting with her boss.

"Shit!" she exclaimed, dashing toward the elevator. "I've got to go."

"Wait—"

"I'm late!" She jabbed at the elevator button, thankful that, for once, she didn't have to wait forever for the doors to open.

"Lori—"

"I've got to go!" She pressed the floor for the garage repeatedly. "My boss. I need to go."

"Can I—"

The elevator doors shut before he could finish his question

CHAPTER 3

Logan

THE SILVER PANELS slid shut before he could finish asking Lori if he could make up for the unfortunate dick pic situation by buying her dinner.

Or maybe a year's worth of dinners.

Fuck, what had he been thinking?

He *hadn't* been thinking. Which was precisely the problem. He'd been near delirious from not sleeping fully for days and add in four, no *five* beers and he'd been blitzed out of his mind.

Stumbling back to his apartment, thinking of that little smirk Hannah had sent him before she'd gone. *"Send something to relax me later."*

None of that meant a fucking picture of his cock.

With his face in it.

No, he didn't go around sending random photographs of his private parts to women he'd just meant—or as it turned out, women he'd never met who turned out to be beautiful and funny and smelled incredible . . . *and* lived next door.

Fuck.

Okay, so he didn't have a *lot* of experience sending dick pics. None, actually.

But even drunk, he should have had some fucking sense.

Moron.

He hit the button for the elevator, waited a godawful long time for the car to come, then got on and headed out to explore the new city that was going to be his home.

Logan was going to beat this jet-lag, dammit.

First stop was to take a Lyft down to the waterfront and see Pier 39. He'd never been to San Francisco before, having grown up in the mid-west before joining the military and spending most of his time in Germany, Japan, and then various bases across the States. But he'd never been to San Francisco. So, when his brother had moved out of his apartment in the city and had needed to sub-let the space, Logan had jumped on the opportunity to spend his first few months out of the military somewhere new.

Somewhere to reset.

To figure out what the fuck he was going to do with his life.

He had some technical skills, but what he actually enjoyed? He was . . . drawing a blank.

That was the confusing and frustrating part.

He'd been competent for fifteen years and now he had to figure out the next chapter of his life. No pressure, no big deal.

Sighing, Logan thanked the driver then got out of the car. Immediately, he was blasted with surprisingly cold air, the wind whipping through his coat and hair. It wasn't as frosty as a German winter, but it was a damn lot colder than he'd expected for California.

Fog curled around the buildings, the bay was churned up into heavy waves, and even though it was relatively early on a weekday, the pier was busy.

He wove his way through the crowded boardwalk, taking in the myriad of shops with racks of sweatshirts lined up in front of their doors—a smart business move as far as he was concerned, based on the wind and fog. But there weren't just T-shirt and souvenir and sock shops, there were also galleries and candy shops with huge drums full of salt-water taffy and root beer barrels and ribbons of colorful, twisted sugar.

But it didn't take long for him to reach the end of the shops and slip through an opening that led to a wooden walkway surrounding the perimeter.

Here was the part he liked.

Actually being able to hear the waves crashing against the support posts, the barking of the sea lions as they alternately lounged and jostled for prime position on the floating platforms in the water. There were only a few other people walking or taking in the view, mostly older folks or couples sneaking in an early lunch.

Here he could smell the tang of fish.

Here he could hear the waves.

Here he could feel a bit more like himself.

Logan stood for a few moments, watching the sea lions, enjoying the breeze and the fact that he didn't have anything pressing on his time.

He could binge bad TV all day, wander around the city for hours, go to bars, get numbers from beautiful women, and . . . send random dick pics.

Groaning, he pulled his cell from his pocket and took a photo of the sea lions, then one of fog-enshrouded Alcatraz in the distance, which made him suddenly have the urge to watch that old Nick Cage movie, *The Rock*. Well, know what? Once the cable guys came that afternoon, he *could* watch it. He had *all* day to watch. He had *six* months to watch it. He—

Was going to go absolutely insane unless he found some-thing to do.

For nearly all of the last fifteen years, he'd been told when to get dressed, what job to do, when to eat, when to go to bed.

Now five days of freedom, and he was losing his mind.

But all Logan could picture were endless blank days of

waking up and wandering around or watching TV until the sun set and he got tired enough to sleep.

What a prime catch he was, having this much of a pity party.

Deliberately, he pulled up the app on his phone and scheduled a ride to take him back to the apartment. It was time he pulled his shit together and began figuring out what the rest of his life would entail.

He strode to the front of the pier, just as his car pulled up, and got in, making small talk for a minute or two before the driver went quiet.

That quiet was what did him in.

Though this time, it didn't involve nudity.

Or, well, of the human variety.

Though the object in the shot wasn't wearing pants. Thankfully, the pant-less state wasn't illegal, as it was a sea lion that was making a comical face as it was knocked off the platform.

He pulled up his text chain with Lori, added the photo, then sent,

Sorry I made you late.

Then he rode back to his apartment, vowed to never send another dick pic, and immersed himself in the want ads.

———

BY THAT AFTERNOON, still Lori hadn't texted back. Not to his picture, nor the message from the night before. Which, in fairness, he hadn't really expected, considering she was both at work and their first go at texting hadn't exactly been great.

Well, for her.

For *him*, he couldn't get her out of his mind.

She'd been so fucking cute when he'd deserved a verbal thrashing. Then funny enough to make his drunk ass laugh, then sober up rapidly when she'd rightfully called him out after that. Beyond all of that, she was gorgeous. And . . . she was his neighbor.

Fucking hell.

He'd sent a dick pic to Brandon's neighbor.

His brother was going to kill him. Especially, when he'd gotten an email just that morning telling Logan to keep it in his pants and give Lori her distance.

Thrusting a hand through his hair, Logan pushed up from the sofa and set his laptop to the side.

He'd spent several hours going through the online classifieds, trying to find anything that might excite him enough to want to spend the second half of his life doing it.

And . . . nothing.

Plus, it wasn't like the sniper skills he'd learned in military were particularly useful, unless he wanted to be a police officer or private security.

Did he want to be a cop? Not really. Private security? Even less appealing.

Firefighting? Maybe, but he'd need to go back to school—

School.

Maybe that was the answer.

If so, what would he study?

Another question.

Because even if he did want to be a firefighter, he didn't think he'd pass the physical. The piece of shrapnel in his hip ensured that.

He'd recovered, mostly, but he couldn't make a day-to-day career out of lifting people or dragging hoses around. A year ago, before the IED had gone off, then sure. Now, not so much.

Logan shook his head, not letting the memories take him back under.

He was in a good place finally. He'd been lucky when several others hadn't.

And so he had a duty to move on.

Sighing, he continued pacing and found that the movement didn't give him any answers.

School.

Yes. That felt right. He should focus on that.

Figure out what he should study, use it as an opportunity to move forward.

Good. Great.

But *what* to study?

Only one thing came to mind. One subject he'd always enjoyed. Biology.

But he was going to be downright elderly sitting in those chairs surrounded by eighteen-year-olds.

And what else did he have to do that was better?

Sit around his brother's place for days on end brooding?

"Fucking hell, man," he muttered, striding to the window and deliberately ignoring both the pain in his hip and his heart. Both would abate. Move on.

Move *forward*.

Because that was what this was about.

He needed to move forward when all he wanted to do was look back.

He went back to the computer and started filling out college applications.

CHAPTER 4

Lorelai

Lᴏʀɪ ᴄᴀᴍᴇ out of the elevator at the end of the day a hell of a lot slower than she'd left. Her backpack felt like it weighed a hundred pounds, her brain was fuzzy from the lack of sleep, and . . .

Logan had texted her another picture.

She was scared to open it.

Snorting, she knew she was less scared to see the picture and more frightened that if she looked at it and liked it then she'd suddenly find herself next door, sampling the goods she'd seen in that first picture, and thus, ending her very long celibacy streak.

Not that she was opposed to ending it.

Just the reason she *hadn't* was because normally she was extremely picky.

Who was she kidding?

A man who looked like Logan? No red-blooded, straight, single female was going to turn him down, photo faux pas or not.

Still, she'd had a day. Heather had been understanding,

albeit not pleased to be kept waiting, and throughout their meeting Lori had felt like a misbehaving child in the principal's office.

Thankfully, the program she'd been working on had demonstrated beautifully, with absolutely no hitches on her part.

The rest of the day hadn't gone smoothly though.

She'd spilled coffee on herself, accidentally and permanently deleted several important lines of code for a different project, whose deadline was rapidly approaching. At which point, she'd christened everyone within earshot with her favorite set of curse words. Unprofessional, yes, but uncommon? No. Unfortunately for Lori, Heather O'Keith's nephew, Hunter, had been visiting the office. He'd heard her then had joyfully repeated the slew of f-words the entire way down the hall, much to his mother, Abby's, displeasure.

Pissing off *all* the O'Keiths today.

Way to go, her.

She reached the front door of her condo and wrestled her key into the lock. The damn thing always stuck, and then add in the heavy wood and her oversized backpack, and it was a struggle to get into her place on a good day.

Today, with her fuzzy brain, it was not her finest moment.

And it got worse.

"Here," Logan said, "Let me help you."

One arm reached down to snag the keys from her hand, and suddenly she was ensconced in yummy, spicy male.

Come on, universe. Throw me a bone here.

It did, her brain reminded her. *Last night.*

She snorted as Logan easily twisted the key in the lock—big hands—and then effortlessly pushed open her door, holding it wide so she could slip inside.

"Thanks," she said, dropping her bag on the floor then leaning back against the heavy wooden panel.

"No problem." He let go and turned to leave. Randomly, she noticed he had a jacket on. Was he going out to another bar to find another beautiful Hannah who rattled his brains enough to send her naked pictures?

Lori bit her lip, indecision warring within her before she just decided to go with her gut.

"Oh, hey, Logan?" she asked, not wanting him to leave even though she didn't exactly understand the reason why. "How did you end up in Brandon's condo?"

Logan grinned. "Brandon's my brother. When he got the contract to work in Germany, he threw me a solid and let me stay since I've never been to San Francisco."

Two thoughts went through her mind.

First, how in God's green earth were Logan and Brandon related?

Second, *he was Brandon's brother?*

Okay, so really, they were just one looping thought, but still.

How was that possible?

Not that Brandon wasn't attractive. He was. But he was also five-seven, maybe a hundred and fifty pounds on a good day, had white-blonde hair, pale blue eyes, and—

"Are you the milkman's baby?" Lori blurted.

Then immediately gasped and threw her hands over her mouth.

Logan grinned. "Nope. Full related by blood."

"I'm sorry," she said, and the apology was muffled by her fingers, so she peeled them back and tried again. "I'm sorry. That was exceptionally rude."

"Not the first time I've heard it," he said, leaning back against the door frame and pulling out his cell. "And it won't be the last. If I didn't know my mom as well as I do, I would definitely think I was adopted or hatched out of an egg or something. See?" He held up the phone and instinctively, she jerked back.

He dropped his hand, smile chagrined. "I deserved that."

Lori shook her head. "No, sorry. That was my fault."

"Want to see my family?"

"Are you all clothed?" she asked tentatively.

He glared.

"Okay," she said. "They're clothed. Why don't you come in for a second? My feet are killing me."

Logan glanced at her shoes. "Um . . ."

Her fancy sneakers. She shrugged, tone a little defensive. "They're my special tennies, and not broken in."

One brow came up.

She got irritated and let go of the door. "This, sir, is a judgment-free zone." Lori spun and started down the hall of her condo.

The day had been a day, and so now she was going to put on her pajamas, order a pizza, and watch a movie. Her cell would be on Do Not Disturb and she was going to get a full night's sleep so tomorrow wouldn't be as life-y as today.

There.

Good plan.

Done.

The door closed as she was shoving her fancy sneakers into the closet in her hallway.

"I hope the offer to come in is still good," he said from a few feet behind her.

She sniffed, brushed by him and hefted her backpack, taking it to the kitchen counter and going through her usual post-work process of plugging in her laptop, unloading the snacks she'd hoarded home from the office, and then extracting her cell.

"Do you like pepperoni?" she asked.

Logan's face warmed. "Yup."

"Good," she muttered and spent the next half minute putting in an order for pizza before setting her phone on the counter. "Drink?"

He nodded. "Sure, thanks."

She walked to the fridge and handed him a beer. "I'm putting on my pajamas and this is *not* an opportunity for you to get a real-time view of anything that I might sext."

There. Told off.

"Lori?"

She paused in the doorway to her bedroom. "Hmm?"

"Did *you* want a drink?" he asked.

Oh. That was nice. She wrinkled her nose, not wanting nice, wanting to hold on to her irritation, however unreasonable it was.

And let it be stated for the record, that she knew it was incredibly unreasonable to be annoyed because someone had misjudged her fancy sneakers.

It was just . . . the day had been a *day*.

"I have wine back at my place, if you prefer that."

Ugh. Fine. That was nice as well as sweet.

She sighed, let go of her irritation. "I'd love a beer. I promise I'll be more human by the time I put my pajamas on. It's just been a . . ."

"Day?" he finished when she trailed off.

Her lips twitched. "Yup. *That*."

"Okay, well, I'll attempt to make your day better by opening you a beer." He paused, head cocking to the side. "I can also leave, if that's better for you."

More nice. More wrinkling of her nose.

"No," she said. "I'd like for you to stay. Brandon and I used to hang out a lot. I've missed that." Lori pushed into her bedroom. "I'll be back in five minutes."

Closing and locking the door behind her, she headed to her closet. The very day-y day was going to get better.

She knew it.

CHAPTER 5

Logan

HE SPUN to the fridge and pulled out a beer for Lori, thinking that the contents inside mirrored what he'd filled Brandon's with, although his had more vegetables.

Lori appeared to only have an assortment of beer, ketchup, and mustard.

Logan pulled open the freezer. And ice cream.

A *lot* of ice cream.

He grinned and shut the freezer then went to sit at the dining room table where she'd dropped a mound of protein bars, bagged popcorn, freeze dried fruit, and several small cans of Diet Coke.

Quite a haul.

No wonder her backpack had been weighing her down.

Or maybe that was just her day, because he'd gotten her started off on the wrong foot.

Fuck. Guilt sucked.

But then again, after having come out of the IED mostly unscathed when several of his friends hadn't, Logan knew all about guilt.

He heard the lock on the bedroom door just before it opened and Lori walked out. How in the hell she made a baggy sweatshirt and pink printed unicorn pajama bottoms look sexy was a feat of nature. But she did.

His cock twitched. Pathetic.

"Beer?" he asked, holding it out.

She nodded and took it, leading them over to the couch and sitting down. He sat on the opposite end.

"Can I see that picture of your family?"

Logan grinned. "Sure that's the one you want to see?"

A huffed-out laugh. "Yes, I'm sure."

He pulled out his cell, unlocking it to show her the photo of him, Brandon, and their parents the last time they were all together. Logan towered over all of them, and his coloring was completely different.

Which is why he wasn't the least bit offended when Lori lifted her eyes from the screen and said, "Can we circle back to the milkman's baby?"

"No." He laughed, flicked a finger so another pic came up on the screen. "My grandfather," he said when she glanced up at him, question in her eyes.

"Oh."

"Yeah."

"I'm an only child," she said. "My parents retired to Florida, but I grew up here." A shake of her head. "Sorry, that was a weird transition. I feel like my brain works in tangents sometimes. A line heading toward infinity then jumping onto a completely other one, heading another direction."

Logan smiled. "I have to admit, I'm kind of digging the zigzags."

She giggled. "That is almost verbatim what Brandon used to say."

Which was the moment he realized she'd mentioned Brandon several times now, and he didn't have any understanding at all of what Brandon was to her. Had they been dating? Friends? Was Brandon interested in her?

Shit. What if his brother wanted Lori?

He couldn't—

"It's also one thing my fiancé hated about me," she said and sighed, taking a long swig of the beer. "Obviously, he became my ex." Her smile was tight. "But because he became my ex, I also got to meet your brother."

Logan's gut tightened. "Oh. Did you two—"

"No." She shook her head. "God *no.*"

Now his gut tightened for a different reason. His brother may not be the most built or outgoing guy in the world, but he was good and smart and—

"Brandon's girlfriend Cassie is absolutely perfect for him. In fact, things got so serious right before he moved that I went from having two buddies most weeknights to no buddies." Her lip stuck out. "Both of my best friends moved to Germany. Brandon for work. Cassie because she decided—rightfully—she couldn't be without Brandon for a year."

"I—Cassie?"

She frowned. "You didn't know your brother had a girlfriend?"

More tightening. And who was the asshole now?

"No," he said. "Brandon never said anything."

"Hmm."

Familiar guilt reared its head. "Not his fault," Logan said. "I've been . . . out of contact for a lot of the last year."

Lori set her beer down. "What does that mean?"

He sighed. "I was in the military. Last year, I was in an accident. An IED went off near—"

She gasped. "Oh my God. Are you okay?" She patted his arm, pulled back. "Of course, you're okay. I'm sorry. I—"

Logan covered her hand with his. "I'm fine. I had some friends who aren't."

Her eyes dropped to her lap, but not before he saw them fill with moisture. "I'm sorry. That's horrible."

"It is," he said. "It's our job. It's part of the risk we accept, but it is also really hard to lose people you consider family." He sucked in a breath, released it slowly, tucking those memories back down. "I was hurt, and it took me some time to recover in Germany."

She nodded. "So, that's why he applied for the job."

"Brandon?" Another nod. "Yeah, I think so. We just didn't think by the time his German visa was processed that I'd be home. I think we overlapped for all of a week and most of that was filled with my appointments and debriefings."

"Cassie didn't leave to join him until a few days ago. I'm guessing that's why—" He nodded as Lori did that nose-wrinkling thing that was absolutely adorable. "I wonder why he didn't tell me about you, though."

"My fault," Logan admitted. "I didn't want anyone outside our family to know. Stupid, but"—he sighed—"it felt like my whole life had been determined by the military and then suddenly I was injured and forced to be discharged. I didn't want to be someone's pity case of a brother. I just wanted to be left alone and—"

She tugged her hand back. "And now I'm forcing you to rehash it."

"No," he said. "The psychologists did that. My parents and Brandon did it. I'm in a better place than I was six months ago, but I still definitely feel like my life has taken a sharp left I hadn't prepared for."

"Did you always want to be a soldier?"

He nodded. "Joined the army straight out of high school. Been in ever since." A sigh. "Thought I'd retire in uniform."

"I'm sorry."

Logan picked up his beer. "Stupid to be upset about something I can't change. Especially when that something isn't loss of life or limb, like—"

He cut himself off with a sip.

Lori touched his arm, pretty eyes locked on his for a long moment. She didn't tell him she was sorry again, or give any other platitudes. Instead, she leaned up, wrapped her arms around his shoulders, and hugged him tight.

Everything inside Logan relaxed at the contact.

The past disappeared. The hurt faded to an ache.

The only thing that mattered was how good Lori felt against him, how incredible she smelled, how nice it felt to have someone to hold him.

"My bad day suddenly seems less life-y," she murmured.

He grinned, leaned back when she dropped her arms. "*This* is what I was looking for last night in the bar."

"A hug?"

He shook his head. "A distraction. Some comfort. Someone to talk to."

Lori had tears in her eyes, but he watched her blink them back and smile up at him. "Well, anyone who knows me, knows that I can talk with the best of them. So, for as long as you're around, you'll be stuck talking to me."

Logan opened his mouth to say that being stuck with anything—talking, hugging, texting, whatever—with Lori wasn't a trial in the least, but then the buzzer rang, and she popped off the couch to answer it.

Then spent the next five minutes bringing the pizza and plates and napkins in, dishing up slices, then consulting him on what movie to watch.

Eventually, they settled on an action flick they'd both already seen.

But that worked for him, because Logan got to hear her commentary on why the hero was failing, ask questions to get her fired up enough to go off on one of those tangents her ex had supposedly hated, but that he found extremely charming, and he got to spend time with a beautiful—where it mattered most, on the inside—woman.

By the time he went back to Brandon's condo, he was happy and relaxed and so full of pizza and beer that he didn't have any problems falling asleep.

And because of that, he didn't see Lori's reply to his picture until the morning.

I think I like the first pic better.

But he did see it first thing in the morning.

And because of *that*, for the first time in more than a year, he went about his day with a smile on his face.

CHAPTER 6

Logan: You're not late today are you?
Lori: Nope. No a-holes made me sleep through my alarm.
Logan: Maybe you need a louder alarm?
Lori: *eye roll emoji* Nice try, buster.
Logan: Want to have dinner at my place tonight? I saw your fridge. It's in desperate straights.
Lori: Does that mean you're buying?
Logan: If you steal some more of those chocolate-covered pretzel things from your work then, yes, I'm buying.
Lori: Good. Pick what you want to eat and get two. I'll eat anything except for mushrooms.
Lori: *shuddering GIF*
Logan: Anything?
Lori: Anything aside from fungi.
Logan: Anchovies?
Lori: Sure.
Logan: Oysters.
Lori: Both raw and Rockefeller.
Logan: Olives.
Lori: Yup. I especially like putting them on all my fingers and then eating them off one by one.

Logan: Lori.

Lori: What?

Logan: That's worse than my picture.

Lori: Um. No. Nice try.

Logan: I'm imagining you sucking them off and—

Logan: I'm stopping there.

Lori: . . . I. Can't. Breathe.

Logan: I didn't mean it like that.

Lori: Uh-huh. Sure.

Logan: Stop laughing or no pasta for you.

Lori: Carbs?

Logan: If you behave yourself. I was also going to get dessert.

Lori: Chocolate carbs, please.

Logan: Will you be on your best behavior?

Lori: No promises. But I won't send you naked pictures.

Logan: Not going to live that down ever, am I?

Lori: Nope. But I promise to keep it a private joke between us.

Logan: Good. Then I'll get you chocolate and carbs.

Lori: And chocolate carbs?

Logan: *sends photo of the dessert case at the bakery* Keep it between us and you can pick your poison.

Lori: All of them.

Lori: Just kidding. That chocolate cheesecake on the left.

Logan: Done. 6pm work?

Lori: I'll be there with bells on.

Logan: All I'm asking is for you . . . and your fancy sneakers.

Lori: *glarey eyes emoji*

Lori: Gotta go back to work. See you later.

CHAPTER 7

Lorelai

LOGAN DELIVERED ON THE CHEESECAKE, and she came wearing pajamas paired with her fancy sneakers. The pasta he'd had DoorDashed was delicious, and they put another movie on, but same as the night before, they spent more time gabbing than actually watching it. She'd gone home late and then crashed headlong into sleep. No more mid-night wake-ups, no more sleeping through her alarm.

They'd done the same thing at her place the next night.

Then back to his after that.

Then repeated the pattern, trading off with hosting dinners every night for the next few weeks.

Lori loved every minute of their time together. It was mostly like having Brandon back, the easy rapport between her and Logan making her wonder if conversation skills ran in the Smith family or if Logan and Brandon had both just lucked out.

Of course, the *mostly*-like-having-Brandon-back part stemmed from the fact that Logan was his brother.

And also because she didn't want to jump Brandon's bones, like she did Logan's.

Not that Brandon was unattractive, because he was certainly good-looking. But there wasn't a spark, and the entire time they'd known each other, she'd been with someone, or after The Dumping that had left her crying in the hall and had provoked Brandon to have her over for the first time, she'd been in recovery mode. Then by the time she'd able to end her hiatus of self-imposed social distancing, he'd been with Cassie.

No opportunity. No interest.

That was mutual.

But he was a damned good friend, along with Cassie.

Although, he was also damn good friend who hadn't shared the information about Logan's injury and recovery.

Though, based on what Logan had said, it hadn't been Brandon's information to share.

Sigh.

She'd need to talk it out with Brandon.

Hard of late, with the time difference. Every time they got a few minutes on the phone, he'd had to run off to bed or she'd been blearily just awake. She was going to have to put her concerns in email form, but for now, she'd just focus on the fact that it felt nice to have a friend next door again and not that Brandon hadn't shared, or that she'd dreamed about his brother the night before.

Lie. She'd dreamed about him for *all* of the nights before.

Or rather, a very specific part of Logan.

Pervert.

As in, *she* was the pervert this time.

But it had been a very good dream, one that involved her having multiple orgasms courtesy of that giant cock.

Yum.

If only Logan had been giving her signals that he might be interested.

Instead, he'd seemed to step into Brandon's role and been carefully keeping distance between them.

Which proved he wasn't the huge dick—no pun intended—

that his text messages had first presented him as . . . but she already knew that. He'd shown that within a few minutes of them meeting in person. He didn't need to keep proving he was a good guy.

In fact, she'd like some of that dick to—

Stop.

She'd been missing Brandon and Cassie, now she had Logan. Maybe he simply wasn't interested in her as more than a friend.

Well, that wasn't a maybe.

That was a certain.

He'd held doors for her, occasionally touched her arm. He texted funny stuff, saw her every night. He knew about her ridiculously happy parents, her double major in math and computer science. She knew about his favorite movies, that his injury had been to his hip, that he'd decided to go back to school and study biology.

But there wasn't an undercurrent of heat between them.

She might have longing, but he wasn't carrying a torch for her.

Stifling a sigh, she reached to pick up her plate, but Logan nudged her away. "I got them. It's late and you've got that that important work meeting tomorrow."

It was true she was meeting with Heather again the next day, but—

"I can help—"

He nodded to the door. "Shoo."

"I should—"

The plate dropped to the table. "Lori." He sighed.

Her brows drew together. "What's the matter?"

His chin dropped to his chest, a long, slow breath escaped his lips. "Lori, honey," he murmured. "You need to go."

Her heart skipped a beat at the endearment. "I can wash—"

Hot brown eyes flew up to meet hers. "Go."

She shook her head, not certain why he was upset—

"Lori." It sounded like it was ground out between his teeth.

"What? What did I do?"

"Fuck." He thrust his hands into his hair, turned and paced away, eyes on the window. She crossed to him, placed a hand on his arm. His head whipped around so fast that she took several steps back. He looked absolutely furious. "I'm trying to be good here, Lori. I've spent the last few weeks dreaming of you, wanting you, jerking off to the mental image of stripping those ridiculous pajamas off your sexy body. I get that you don't want me, but—"

"*What?*"

"I know you want me to be a friend, like Brandon was," he said, turning around to face her. "But I can't just be around you all the time and not want to—" Logan paced away again.

"You want me?"

Brown eyes over his shoulder. "Go, Lori."

"But I thought you didn't want *me*." She strode around in front of him, shoving him back lightly. "I've been over here every night in my fancy sneakers and you've been friend-zoning the shit out of me."

"Um, no," he said. "You've been friend-zoning *me*."

"Uh, no. I'm the one having wet dreams about you every night."

He frowned. "Can girls have wet dreams?"

She rolled her eyes. "That's your response to me telling you that?"

Lips twitching, he said, "I take it back."

"Good."

"Good." His eyes bored into hers, and it was as though he'd finally pulled back a veil, revealing heat he'd kept banked over the last few weeks. "I don't want to be your friend, sweetheart."

She nibbled at her bottom lip. "What *do* you want to be?"

"More."

Lori dropped her gaze to her feet for a moment. "A boyfriend?"

"Yes."

"*Friend* friend?"

"Yes, that, too."

Her heart rolled over in her chest, exposing itself. Could she do this? She wanted to, but should she? She glanced up, saw the warmth in his eyes, and figured if she didn't, she'd regret it for the rest of her life. "How about a provider of chocolate carbs?"

Amusement crept into his tone, and he said, "Yes."

"Good."

She launched herself into his arms and slanted her mouth across his.

CHAPTER 8

Logan

HER MOUTH MET HIS, and heat exploded down his spine. He didn't think, just reacted, wrapping his arms around her waist, hauling her up against him, and kissing her exactly as he'd been dreaming up for weeks now.

It was better than he could have imagined.

Her lips were soft, her mouth was slick and hot, and her tongue met his stroke for stroke.

Eventually, though, he had to pull back to breathe.

"Logan," she murmured, when their lips parted.

He knew the feeling. His lungs were screaming, but his mind was demanding *more, now*.

"Lori," he groaned, dragging his mouth along her jaw, tracing it along the shell of her ear, noting that she shivered when he made it to the spot just behind it. Then her fingers were in his hair, and she was yanking his head so their mouths met again, and they kissed and kissed and kissed.

Her hands slipped under the hem of his T-shirt, nails dragging along his back. "Off," she demanded, yanking it up and because it was fewer clothes rather than more, he broke their mouths apart and tugged it over his head. Hers was next, Lori grabbing the bottom and pulling it off without ceremony. It landed on the floor next to his, but when she made to reach for the button on her jeans, he stopped her.

"Hey," he murmured. "I don't think—"

"I want you, Logan Smith," she said. "So, I guess the question is do *you* want to stop?"

He froze for a heartbeat before his lips curved. He didn't think he would ever be able to predict what this woman was going to say. "I don't want to stop."

"Good." A beat. "Do you have a condom?"

"Yup."

"Good." Her fingers flicked open the button on her jeans, tugged at the zipper, and shoved them down her legs. They tangled at her ankles and she teetered, but Logan lurched forward to grab her, sweeping her up into his arms. "The one time I don't change into pajamas," she muttered.

"I happen to like that ass in jeans," he murmured, shifting her weight as he walked so he could help her untangle the denim from her ankles.

"Pajamas would make for easier access."

"Sometimes easy access isn't everything."

She paused, eyes coming up to meet his, lips curving. "True."

He got the jeans off the other foot and let them fall to the floor, and then he had his arms full of beautiful woman, breasts encased in black lace, pussy in . . .

"Are those unicorns?"

Her cheeks flared red, but she didn't look away. "Unicorns happen to be very sexy," she grumbled.

Considering they were on the woman he was crazy about, Logan wasn't going to argue. Instead, he tossed Lori onto the bed, followed her down, and let his mouth tell her exactly how much he enjoyed them.

She tasted of honey and sunshine.

Her skin was silk.

Her breasts . . . well, he lost his mind for a bit there, kissing and sucking at the pebbled tips, kneading the round globes, licking and tasting and laving every inch of them. And then every inch of *her*.

Her pussy tasted like honey, too.

And he couldn't get enough, using his tongue on her labia, pressing and flicking it against her clit, slipping a finger inside her until he found a rhythm that had her hips jerking up and pleadings escaping her lips in gasped exhales.

"Logan— *oh*. Fuck," she groaned, head writhing on the pillow. "Yes. Like that. No, faster. Yes. That. Don't stop. Don't stop. Don't—"

She broke off with a long keening moan, pussy convulsing around his fingers.

Logan's head was spinning, the taste of her on his tongue, her scent in his nose, his cock ready to break in half, but he paused, waited for her eyes to flutter open.

"Are—"

Lori reached for the button of his jeans . "Inside me. Now."

He didn't need to be told twice, extracting the condom from his wallet, brushing her hands away, unbuttoning and pushing his jeans down before rolling it on. Twenty seconds later, he was between her thighs and pushing home.

Fucking. Best. Thing. Ever.

She was tight. She was hot. She was—

Lori kissed him.

—everything.

He moved, thrusting in and out, desire spiraling out from his cock and shooting down his spine. It was absolutely the best thing he'd *ever* felt. In fact, it was so good that he didn't even register the fact that his hip was twinging.

Logan couldn't feel anything except him, Lori, and the magic they were making.

He didn't last long.

But luckily, neither did she.

Thirty seconds later, he slipped a hand between them, finding a spot that made her arch and cry out, pussy clenching around him as she toppled over the edge.

He was right behind her.

He'd started the night thinking he'd be getting nothing more than friendship with Lori and trying to convince himself that it was all she was willing to give, and so he needed to be content with it.

He ended the night pulsing inside her.

Life had dealt him another sharp left.

But this time, he didn't mind.

The morning, however, wouldn't be so kind.

———

"I'M LATE!" Lori shot out of bed, completely naked, hair an absolute mess, and ass shaking in his face.

Best. View. Ever.

But then he processed what she'd said.

Shit. *Fuck.*

He'd screwed her over again with another meeting for her boss.

"Here," he said, leaping out of bed and making a mad dash for her clothes. "Get dressed, get to the office. I'll go next door and get your laptop and drop it with a change of clothes later."

The panic disappeared, relief taking its place. She leaned toward him, pressed her mouth to his for a brief second. "You're the best, Logan Smith."

"Go," he said. "There's a spare toothbrush in the drawer next to the sink."

He threw on a pair of sweats as she ran into the bathroom then hustled to grab her purse and her cell, putting both where she couldn't miss them by the front door. A moment later, he grabbed the spare key to her place that Brandon had hanging in his hall closet, and was out in the hall.

And running straight into Brandon.

Who had a beautiful blonde standing behind him, one who was apparently madly in love with his brother, but who Logan hadn't known about until Lori had mentioned her.

Secrets. His brother was all about the secrets.

"Whoa, Log," Brandon said.

"Hey," Logan said. "I'm happy to see you, but just a second. Lori needs—"

Hip twinging, he'd definitely overdone it on round two the previous night, he darted across the hall, opened Lori's door then spent the next few minutes dashing around her place and shoving things into her backpack. Clothes, underwear, fancy sneakers, laptop. All check.

Then he hustled out, thinking maybe he could catch her before she'd gone.

Instead, when he came out, the elevator doors were closing, Lori presumably within them, and his brother was glaring at him from his condo's door with crossed arms. "What the fuck, dude?"

Logan sighed and pushed past him, heading toward the bedroom to put on a shirt and shoes.

Cassie, or at least that was who he assumed the blonde was, was standing uncomfortably in the hall, and he paused.

"Hi," he said. "I'm Logan. Come in"

"Cassie," she murmured as she and his brother trailed him into the condo.

"I'll be right back," he said, moving toward the bedroom.

She nodded, glanced uneasily from Logan to Brandon.

A few minutes later, Logan was dressed, teeth brushed, and facing a pissed off older brother.

"What in the fuck are you doing with Lori?" Brandon snapped

Logan stifled a sigh, decided to counter-attack. "Why didn't you tell me about Cassie?"

Brandon's teeth clicked together.

"I know you two are friends," Logan said. "But I like Lori, a lot."

Brandon sniffed. "Sure, you do. I know all about how you *like* women," he muttered.

"Because you saw me trying to cope when the worst shit of my life happened. Yes, I was drinking. Yes, I was fucking. Yes, I was absolutely out of my mind." He sucked in a breath. "Look. I know we both hold a lot of stuff to our chests, but I'm not the asshole I was a year ago. I fully admit I was a fucking mess then. I didn't know what I was doing. Who I was any longer. My friends were severely injured or dead and—"

Cassie gasped.

Logan dropped his chin to his chest. "I'm sorry. I shouldn't have said it that way—"

She crossed over to him. "Logan. *No.* Oh my God, I'm sorry. I—"

Brandon touched her shoulder, tugged her back. "Hey, I get it. You were running." He glanced down at Cassie. "That seems to be a Smith trait, but that doesn't mean you're good enough for Lori. She's my best friend, and her ex was an asshole. She deserves someone who isn't bogged down by the past, who can live in the present. No offense, Log, but you've got a lot of baggage."

He did.

That much was true.

"And I know Lori is beautiful and convenient but—"

"I love her."

Both Cassie and Brandon's mouths fell open.

But it was the gasp in the hallway that set his heart sinking.

Lori was there, Brandon's condo door wide open, her face pale, keys dangling from her fingers. "I-I sh-shouldn't have heard t-that," she stammered. "I'll g-go." She spun around and ran .

The backpack hit the ground as he chased after her, snagging her arm just as she made it to the hall.

"Shit, Lori," he said. "I didn't mean for you to hear that. It's too soon, I know. I—why are you here?"

She shakily held up her cell. "Heather had to cancel. I figured I'd come back and change." A shuddering breath. "Did you mean it?"

Fuck.

But he couldn't lie to her.

"I did," he said and hurried to add, "I know it's insane. I know we're just starting to learn each other, but Lori, you're the most incredible woman I've ever met. Hands down. I want to learn you more, for us to spend more time together, for you to forget you heard me declare my love so that I can take you somewhere romantic in a reasonable amount of time and tell you then." He cupped her cheek. "I want to do this right with you and—"

"I love you, too," she blurted. "I agree this is insane and too fast and—well, you can just forget you heard it, too"—a smile —"so I can tell *you* again later."

His heart had been pounding out of his chest, but at her words, it relaxed. "Really?"

Her finger came to his lips. "Shh."

"Tell me again."

"Later," she admonished.

And then she dropped her hand to his shoulder and rose on tiptoe. He didn't need any further encouragement. Logan bent his head and kissed her. Then kept on kissing her until Cassie and Brandon came out of the apartment and caught them.

"You boys will talk the rest of this out later," Cassie said, waving as she tugged Brandon toward the elevator.

And Cassie was right.

Brandon and Logan did talk it out later.

In fact, they talked it out so much that Brandon decided that this new Logan, the one who'd decided to go back to school, the one who didn't get drunk in bars any longer, who didn't hide beneath painful memories to keep the world at a distance, was absolutely perfect man for Lori.

EPILOGUE

Lorelai, Two Months Later

SHE WALKED into her condo to find candles on every surface, rose petals on the floor, and . . .

Logan asleep on the couch.

In fairness, she was the one who'd fucked up.

She was supposed to have been home two hours before, but she'd had a problem with one of her programs and had sat down to troubleshoot for *just one minute.*

Well, one had turned into a hundred, and now she was obscenely late.

Two plates were on the table, along with an entire chocolate cheesecake. Her heart pitter-pattered. The man had brought chocolate carbs.

Aw.

She turned, walked over to where Logan was sleeping, the textbook from one of the classes he was taking sprawled across his chest. Carefully, she slid it from him and set it on the coffee table then burrowed her way under his arm.

Even asleep, he still let her in, still hugged her close, still murmured, "I love you."

Just like he did every single time she came to him when he was sleeping.

Whether it was on the couch, like this—though sans candles, cheesecake, and rose petals—or in bed when she worked late. Or even if she got up to get a glass of water or go to the bathroom.

Every time she came back, he whispered, "I love you."

And every time, she whispered back, "I love you, too."

Someday, they would manage to say it again when both of them were awake, or at least *semi*-conscious.

Until then, Lori was just going to let Logan have his moment.

Just hopefully next time she wouldn't be late and ruin it.

Or those glorious chocolate carbs.

BAD MARRIAGE

CHAPTER ONE

Abby

THE BABY WAS CRYING.

Again.

Groaning, she tossed the covers back, pushed herself out of bed, and blearily stood up.

Then promptly tripped over some sort of Lego creation and fell to the carpet.

"Abbs?" came Jordan's groggy voice. "I'll bring Emma to you."

"I'm okay. Go back to sleep," she said, knowing he would do so, and immediately at that. It was almost annoying how quickly the man could slip into unconsciousness.

And he needed it.

Emma had decided it was her tiny six-week-old's task to ensure the entire household was running on fumes—of the energy sense.

Or perhaps the diaper fumes sense.

Snort.

Rolling her eyes at herself, Abby pushed up to her feet, Emma's cries growing in volume with each second that passed.

She stepped over Carter's rendition of a Duplo house this time, snagged her robe from the chair by the door, and slipped out into the hall, still somewhat in awe of how dramatically her life had changed in just a few years.

She had a daughter.

And two sons.

She finally had a family after she'd always felt so lost about her place in the world.

She wouldn't say that her identity was solely based on being a wife and mother, but it had given her the confidence to live out her dreams.

So she could add boss, businesswoman, and partner to her list of attributes.

Along with sleep-deprived.

Pushing into Emma's bedroom, she saw that her daughter was red-faced and squalling—well, she'd heard that last part already, but now she could see the squished-up unhappiness of her expression.

"Oh, baby," she murmured, sweeping over and scooping her up. "I've got you."

The swaddle had come loose, and since Emma's diaper felt full, Abby took her to the changing table and completed the dirty end—literally—of the business. Then re-swaddled her and sat down in the rocker.

Emma had quieted, as she always did once she was picked up, though it was punctuated by tiny cries that told Abby her daughter was hungry. She unsnapped her nightgown and lifted Emma to her breast, rocking her softly and humming a nursery rhyme she didn't know all the words to. Which was okay. Her daughter seemed to like the melody even without the words.

Eventually, Emma finished and lay drowsily in Abby's arms while she tried to summon the energy to cover herself and begin the careful task of setting the baby in the crib without waking her.

Maybe arduous was more like it.

"Here, sweetheart." The soft words had her looking up at her husband, Jordan, who was wearing just a pair of boxer briefs and looking all too much like Thor when she was feeling very blah and stretched out and saggy. He slipped her nightgown back up, buckling the snap with practiced hands. Then he lifted Emma out of her arms.

"I told you to sleep."

"And I told you I'd bring the baby to you," he whispered, pressing a kiss to her forehead. "You're exhausted."

"You've got a membership to that club yourself."

He smiled, and she felt that quirk of his lips like a physical caress, a heat blooming within her that reminded her why they had three small children—though she'd only birthed two of them.

The third, Hunter, they'd adopted. Biologically, he was Jordan's nephew, but in all ways that truly mattered, he was their son.

A son that would need to be driven to school in—she glanced at the clock—three hours.

Dear God.

There was a reason sleep deprivation was considered torture.

She hadn't even realized that her eyes had slipped closed or that Jordan had successfully made the baby-to-the-crib transition until she felt the rocker move, until she felt herself being swept up into his arms.

"Wh—?"

"Hush," he whispered. "The little beast is finally asleep."

She dropped her voice to barely audible. "I'm too heavy."

Flashing blue eyes had her hiding her face in his chest. She hadn't meant to say that out loud, hadn't meant to let the insecurities that were building in her mind outside her brain. She'd just given birth six weeks before. Of course, her body had changed.

"Bull. Shit," he hissed.

She didn't reply, knowing that there wasn't much she could say. She was putting up a good front, but two babies in three years meant that she was feeling more than a little insecure.

Things—skin, breasts, hair—hung differently. Her stomach was . . . well, it might as well be a roadmap for how many lines crisscrossed it.

And she'd lost track of the last time she'd showered or worn a shirt without crumbs or spit-up or poop on it.

Hell, her hair probably had poop in it right now.

A tear leaked out of the corner of her eye.

"Abbs?" Jordan asked softly, navigating the mess of toys like a professional. No Godzilla-esque Duplo destruction for him, that was for sure.

Meanwhile, she—

"Sweetheart," he said, setting her on the bed and wiping the tear—okay *tears*—away. "What is it?"

She shook her head, knowing the inner voice was fueled by exhaustion and hormones. It would pass, and she'd feel more like herself.

Eventually.

"I'm okay," she whispered, hoping eventually would come sooner rather than later.

"You're not," Jordan argued. "But you're also too tired to argue about it now." He swept the covers up and over her, tucking them tightly around her. "Sleep, my love."

"But—"

He slid in next to her, pulled her against his chest. "Sleep."

And truly too exhausted to argue, she did as he ordered.

CHAPTER TWO

Jordan

She looked like a fucking zombie.

Dark circles, shuffling gait, pale skin as she staggered to a chair in the kitchen and sat down.

After making sure it wasn't too hot, he put a mug of tea in front of her and then a plate with toast, cinnamon, and sugar—her favorite of late.

Then he sat next to her.

Tired hazel eyes drifted to his. "Is Hunter up for school?"

He nodded. "I dropped him already."

Those eyes flew to the clock. "I'm sorry," she said. "It was my turn. I must not have heard the alarm and—"

He covered her hand. "I turned off your alarm, sweetheart."

She frowned. "Why?"

"You're not getting enough sleep."

"I'm fine."

He lifted a brow. "We're starting the bottle tonight."

"But—"

"No buts," he said. "You're running yourself ragged between Carter and Hunter and Emma, and you need at least one chunk of solid sleep every night." Squeezing her fingers lightly, he shifted closer to her. "You don't have to be Super Mom. I'm here, too. Let me help."

"But you've been taking more of the nighttime feedings and that isn't fair."

He loved this woman, but she was talking crazy. "You mean I've been carrying Emma around and changing a few diapers while you're *feeding* her," he said. "Tell me which of those is more important."

"Jor."

"I love you," he said. "But this isn't a scoreboard. Your body needs to rest and recover, and you've been pumping, so why not use the milk?"

"What if we need it?"

"More than we both need sleep?"

She froze, and he knew he'd scored a point. Jordan understood she was exhausted—he wasn't feeling particular chipper himself after Emma's weeks of exercising her lungs—but Abby had been through a difficult pregnancy, a difficult delivery, and now a difficult few weeks. She needed more rest than she was getting.

Even if she was trying to pretend otherwise.

"I'm just not sure if it's too soon . . ."

He brushed back her hair from her face. "How about we just try? If it doesn't work out, then we'll go back to the other way."

"Okay," she said and picked up her cup of tea, lifting it to her lips.

Right on cue, Emma, who he'd had set up in the vibrating, musical swing in the corner, began crying. Which was promptly followed by Carter, who had been building a tower of wooden blocks that collapsed.

He glanced at his wife, lips twitching.

"What was that you said about rest?" she asked, fighting a smile.

"We'll look back at these days at some point, right?" He

kissed the top of her head, moved to the swing and picked up Emma, bringing her back to Abby and shifting the mug well out of the way of flailing little arms. Then he scooped up Carter, hugging his son and talking him down from the tower edge before they sat on the rug together and rebuilt an even better one.

"You're a good dad," Abby said, coming over to them and kissing his cheek. "Even if you are a stubborn husband."

"I learned all of my stubborn skills from you," he deadpanned.

She laughed, and even after all these years, it was still the best sound on the planet. "I love you and your stubbornness." A waggling of her brows. "*And* your hammer."

He snorted. "My *hammer* is what got us into this mess."

"True," she said. "But it was worth it."

Jordan stared at his little family—minus one because Hunter was at school—and had to agree.

They were worth every hour of lost sleep and the gray hairs and the vomit and poop and fallen block towers.

———

BUT A WEEK LATER, he had to wonder if Abby felt the same way.

She was getting more sleep, Emma having taken to the bottle like a champ and giving them each a block of almost four hours. It felt like nirvana, like the skies had cleared and the sun was shining down on them.

Or at least it did for him.

Abby had grown steadily quieter, even as the dark circles beneath her eyes faded.

Hormones, perhaps. Or a case of the baby blues. He'd read somewhere that they didn't always come on right after birth, that depression could slide in later.

He made a mental note to keep an extra close eye on her.

He'd just returned from dropping Hunter at school and was looking forward to a nice, hot shower and maybe a cup of coffee sans the side of tears, in that order, so he traversed the stairs as quietly as possible, slipping into the bedroom to not wake the beasts—er, his lovely, beautiful children.

Then tiptoed through the bedroom to not wake his lovely, beautiful *wife*.

He pushed open the door.

Abby was naked and in the shower, her gloriousness visible through the glass panes, and he was abruptly reminded of how long it had been since he'd held his wife, the water pouring down on them, her silken curves against him. She was still the most gorgeous woman he'd laid eyes on, and he needed to hold her. His gaze flicked to the left, to the monitor that showed his younger two children were still sleeping.

And he seized his opportunity.

He stripped down and slid into the shower behind her, slipping his arms around her waist and pulling her back against him.

"Jordan!" she shrieked, trying to squirm away.

"Hi, beautiful," he murmured, flicking his tongue out and tasting the shell of her ear.

"I—" She kept squirming, and he released her, frowning when she stepped out of the spray and reached for the towel hanging over the side, using it to cover herself.

"What is it?"

She shook her head, clutched the towel to her like it was a lifeline and she'd just fallen off a ship in the middle of the ocean. "I—uh—the baby is up." She stepped out of the shower.

Emma wasn't up.

He could see that much, but he could also see that his wife was uneasy about something. Jordan wasn't sure whether she thought he was trying to get lucky—he certainly wouldn't turn her down, but he wasn't expecting anything, especially this soon after she'd given birth—or if she was uncomfortable with her body or if she was still tired and hormonal and just off, but any idiot could see that she needed some space.

"I'll hurry up and shower and grab her," he said, reaching for the bottle of shampoo.

"No!"

His eyes shot to hers, hands covered in suds, soap dripping down his temples.

"I—uh—" She was wrapping her robe around her still towel-covered body. "I've got her."

"Okay, sweetheart," he said.

But inside, he recognized the tell she'd just given him.

And he filed it away to deal with later.

Because he knew exactly how to deal with it.

CHAPTER THREE

Abby

SHE WAS A MESS. An absolute mess.

She was running away from her husband, had jumped like a cat trying to escape a bath when he'd touched her.

Stupid, she knew that.

He'd said time and again she was beautiful . . . but when he'd put his hands on hers, when it had felt different—

She'd just not been able to handle it.

Hustling into the closet, she wrestled her way into her maternity jeans, the stretchy top making her feel like she was trying to squirm into leather leggings for how difficult it was.

Not that she'd ever worn leather leggings.

That was more Seraphina's style.

Her buxom best friend would probably bounce back from pregnancy and slip right into her jeans—or leather leggings.

Meanwhile, Abby was wearing stretch-top clothes and hiding the post-partum bump that still wouldn't go away. Sagging skin, a speed bump, and a husband who looked like a god.

What was she going to do?

The monitor lit up, Carter talking to himself in bed. She watched him, his little feet in the air, kicking back and forth as he chattered. Soon Emma would be awake and hungry, and Abby wouldn't have time for this train of thought, for the nasty thoughts she couldn't seem to stifle in the quiet moments.

She knew they were too harsh, knew she shouldn't think of herself like that.

But she couldn't seem to stop the thoughts from coming.

Especially when Jordan was being so wonderful.

The damned man was being *too* wonderful—taking over the nighttime feeding, bringing her food, doing the laundry and most of the cooking, calling her beautiful, and driving Hunter to school—

With a groan, she yanked a T-shirt out of a drawer and tugged it over her head. Abby knew she was being silly. What sane person complained their partner was doing too much?

The online groups she was part of were filled with posts of men shirking their duties, leaving their wives to fend for themselves with a newborn.

And she was complaining that Jordan was being an actual partner—stepping in when something needed to be done, taking charge of the kids or schedule, not constantly asking her if she needed help.

Instead he was just doing it.

Plates and cups overflowing in the sink? They got washed and put in the dishwasher.

Laundry hampers filled to the brim and then some? They were empty, washed, folded, and put away—more neatly than she could probably do it in her state.

The fridge empty? He got groceries.

The kids were hungry? He cooked.

She'd gotten the fucking Holy Grail of husbands.

And she was absolutely miserable.

Because somehow him being nice and understanding and

responsible, him stepping up without a word from her, made her feel like she wasn't pulling her weight.

She didn't look the same for him any longer *and* she wasn't doing enough.

Double, double, toil and trouble.

"And great," she muttered, hurrying out of the closet and down to Carter's room, "now I'm going as mad as Macbeth and company."

"Mama!" he called, lifting his arms up.

She went over to him, hugging him close. "Hi, my lovely boy," she whispered. "Good morning. You hungry?"

"'Gry!" he exclaimed.

"Should we have bananas and oatmeal?" she asked, grabbing him a set of fresh clothes and getting him ready for the day.

"Yes!"

Emma had begun fussing by the time they emerged into the hall, making animal sounds—"A dog goes woof!"—so they detoured to grab her and then made their way down to the kitchen.

Jordan was on the phone when they came in, and he slipped out with one finger raised, but he'd already prepped the oatmeal with a side of bananas and put her nursing pillow on the table beside her chair.

And her heart squeezed again, guilt sliding through her.

The man was doing too much.

How in the hell was she ever going to make things even between them again?

CHAPTER FOUR

Jordan

HE HUNG up the phone after confirming that the others thought his plan was sound and then went back into the kitchen, ruffling Carter's hair as he determinedly spooned oatmeal into his mouth.

Well, about half of it made it into his mouth.

The rest was on his face and the highchair and his clothes and the floor.

But he loved feeding himself.

Jordan had just gotten in the habit of making twice as much so that a reasonable amount made it into his son's stomach.

Emma was also eating happily, and he sat next to Abby at the kitchen table. "You hungry?"

She bit her lip, nodded. "But I can get it—"

He stood. "Cinnamon toast and tea? Or are you sick of that yet?"

She smiled. "Is it even possible to get sick of cinnamon toast and tea?"

"I'm guessing the correct answer to that question is no."

"Exactly, but Jor—" She stopped. "You really don't have to

wait on me hand and foot. You're already doing so much and—"

"This is my family, sweetheart. I couldn't carry Emma"—he grinned—"and thank God for that, but let me at least take care of you in this way."

Guilt flashed in her eyes. "Are you sure you don't mind?"

"Yes." He tucked a lock of her hair behind her ear. "In fact, it makes me feel like I'm finally doing something productive."

More guilt. "Baby—"

He bopped her lightly on the nose. "Hush."

More guilt in her expression, but Jordan decided not to comment on it or push further. He had a plan, and he was going to stick to it. Or at least, he'd put the plan in place and had to trust that the rest of the Sextant would pull their weight. So, instead of worrying about something he couldn't change, he poured a cup of coffee for himself, brewed her some tea, and then set about spending the rest of the day making sure she got as much rest as possible.

Because his woman had plans that evening.

Whether or not she liked it.

———

SHE WAS GOING to kill him.

They'd been married long enough for him to see that much in her face, but he simply ignored the glare and opened the door a little wider to allow Bec, Sera, CeCe, and Rachel in.

"Hi," CeCe said, kissing him on the cheek and whispering. "Heather's going to call. She's in Berlin."

He smiled. "Thanks for the assist."

"Aunt CeCe!" Hunter yelled, dropping his pencil onto the kitchen counter and tearing through the room to hug Cecilia tight.

"Oof!" she exclaimed, teetering back on her heels before

Jordan snagged her arm to steady her. "How did you get so big?"

"It's my new heart!" he said, or really, yelled, sprinting back to the kitchen, but not before yelling some more—this time over his shoulder, "It makes me a superhero, CeCe!"

"I see that," she said in what someone on the street might think was an indulgent tone.

But Jordan knew better.

Hunter *was* a superhero.

Less of the Hollywood variety and more of the real-life type. He'd been sick for much of his life, and it wasn't until he'd received a heart transplant a few years ago that he'd been able to be a real kid.

It was still hard as hell to let him play sports and skid through the house, especially after Jordan had spent so much time at Hunter's bedside, but Abby was the one who'd actually helped him see that his nephew wouldn't be able to live a full life unless he loosened the protective hold a bit. He'd already been more son than nephew—Hunter's biological dad and Jordan's brother had died before he was born—and Abby, too, had given him the courage to adopt Hunter, to be a true family, and he was forever grateful for her.

And the woman thought she wasn't doing enough?

Ha.

She'd changed his life for the better, made it something he was so damned thankful to be living, made it—

Perfect.

Even with her glaring at him from across the room.

"Where's my little squishy?" Sera asked, hanging her coat on the rack and squeezing Jordan's arm at the same time.

None of the Sextant—and somehow, he'd gotten in the habit of calling Abby and her friends that, even though it was a ridiculous name thought up after too many drinks and an ill-fated Google search—but regardless of that silly name, none of the women were still at guest status, as Abby liked to call it.

They strolled right in, Sera scooping up Carter and kissing his chubby little cheeks, CeCe moving to look at Hunter's homework, Bec grabbing drinks from the fridge and snacks from the pantry, and Rachel carefully snagging Emma from Abby's arms, ordering her to go upstairs for a nap.

"But—"

"But, nothing," Rachel said, in her no-nonsense, efficient tone. "We want to chat and hang out, but not until you've slept a bit more."

"I'm not tired—"

Except, Abby's protest was cut short by a yawn.

Bec, who was setting a pile of snacks on the table, merely raised a brow. "Want to try that line with another group of dirty old ladies?"

Snorting, Jordan moved into the kitchen, grabbing some ingredients for spaghetti, one of the few meals he could cook— and the only one that would work for a large group that Hunter and Carter would both eat as well. But while the cooking was necessary, it was also part distraction.

Letting Abbs' friends take her in hand.

Because sometimes a man needed to call in the experts, and as much as he loved his wife, he knew there were things she still held back from him, still kept close to her chest.

Part because of her asshole of a father.

And part because she felt a responsibility to do everything by herself.

Stubborn woman.

But still, he wouldn't take her any other way. He just knew that sometimes he needed a little help to get through that shell of hers.

When Hunter left to put his homework in his backpack, CeCe came up next to Jordan, leaning a hip against the counter as he sliced vegetables. "It's not often a *man*"—her green eyes danced—"calls an emergency Book Club meeting."

"You mean Wine Club?" he deadpanned.

"Yes, exactly."

He sighed, dropped the veggies into the stockpot. "She says she's not doing enough," he said softly. "Like giving birth and nursing Emma, all while taking care of Hunter and Carter isn't enough."

CeCe snorted.

"Exactly," he said. "But I don't think that's all of it. That's why I called Sera. There's something else going on."

"Yeah?"

He thought about the way she'd jumped away from his touch, the guilt in her eyes, the way she'd avoided being close to him all day.

And his worry was that it was more than being tired or feeling like he was taking on too much. Jordan worried that she was unhappy because of something he was doing and just hadn't found a way to tell him.

Which worried him further.

Because if their communication had broken down that much, if she couldn't just talk to him as a friend and wife, then . . . fuck, he was *definitely* doing something wrong.

Hence the big guns.

Hopefully, if she couldn't talk to him, she would at least talk to her friends.

"We'll sort her out, Jor," CeCe murmured, squeezing his arm. Then she smiled. "After her nap, that is."

"Did Bec get her to go lay down?"

A nod. "Already out, poor thing."

He stirred the pot, began adding tomato sauce. "Emma has decided that sleep is far too overrated."

"I thought you guys were going to hire a nanny."

"Abby wants to wait until she goes back to work."

"A night nurse?"

He shook his head. "Couldn't get her to agree to it."

"Stubborn one, isn't she?"

"It might be her superpower."

CeCe chuckled. "We'll turn the screws, get her to talk."

"How will you torture her?"

"I'll threaten her with a glass of wine," CeCe said.

"That'll do it," he said, feeling better already. Not because of the wine—Abby couldn't stand the stuff, even though the rest of her friends could suck it down like punch—but he felt better because they cared about Abby, because they knew her, because they would help him get to the bottom of this.

And if it ended up that he was the problem that was making his wife so miserable, then Jordan would fix it.

Whatever it was.

CHAPTER FIVE

Abby

BY ALL MEASURES, she should be furious at her husband.

Inviting people over when she was exhausted and had given birth just a few weeks before—six was a few, right?—but regardless, the house was a mess, her body was a mess and—

They were her best friends in all the world.

And Jordan had invited the cackling group of six over *then* had entertained them for a glorious two hours when they'd forced her into a nap.

The house sparkled—or if not that, then it had at least been picked up and organized. How long it would stay that way was questionable, given that it was now home to three kids, but they'd come, they'd cleaned, they'd made her rest, and Jordan had cooked and fed everyone.

Her reheated plate was in front of her, along with a small glass of rum, copiously mixed down with Diet Coke. Sera had said she'd checked the measurements carefully so as not to interfere with her breast milk.

Which was beyond sweet.

Her friend, not the milk. But then again, it wasn't like she went around tasting it. Her milk could be sweet and delicious and—

Her mind threw the brakes on that particular train of thought.

Maybe someone would get their jollies off it, but she'd spent the better part of the last few years feeling like a cow—either because she was nursing or because she was pregnant and as large as one.

It didn't feel very jolly.

Or sweet.

But her friends and Jordan were.

He'd taken the kids upstairs, put the littles to bed, and he and Hunter were camping out in the bedroom rewatching the latest season of *The Mandalorian* before it was his turn to go to sleep.

Abby had to admit she was a little jealous to not be part of the rewatch party—it was so good—but also, it was nice to be hanging with her friends. She'd sat and let the chatter wash over her, a Hallmark movie playing in the background, listening to Bec talk about a new case—and the other lawyer's attempts to circumvent her.

"Which won't work, of course," Bec was saying. "It's practically a juvenile move, and I'd already prepped my clerk to file if he made that move." She cackled and rubbed her hands together. "I only wish I could see his face when that filing goes through."

"You're too smart for your own good," Sera said.

"Nonsense," Heather said, her voice slightly tinny as it came through the speakers of CeCe's phone. She was sitting cross-legged on her bed in Berlin, dressed for the day and wisely abstaining from a drink, as it was breakfast time there. "It's never a bad thing to be smart."

"So says the two smartest women I know," Rachel said.

Bec buffed her knuckles on her chest. "It's a hard cross to bear, that's for sure."

Sera swatted Bec on the shoulder. "Hush you."

"Hey!" Bec swatted her back.

"How's the real estate market right now?" Abby asked quickly, before they could digress too far down the swatting track. She, Bec, and Sera had all been friends since boarding school—and sometimes they still acted like it.

Sera lifted a brow, but her lips were curved. "Putting your mom powers to use?"

"I've become an expert at breaking up fights."

CeCe tsked. "My little squishy and Hunter don't fight. They're angels."

"Hmm," Heather said.

Abby snorted.

Rachel giggled.

And Sera spent the next few minutes telling them about her latest sales—then a few more complaining about a couple of very challenging clients.

After which, Abby tried to turn the conversation to Rachel.

Because if she could just delay enough, give the other women their turn to talk, Heather would have to go to breakfast, and she wouldn't have to give her recap of her life.

Which was a mess.

And not in terms of the state of her house.

Her mind was muddied, tangled and twisted, and she kept going in circles, warring with herself about things she should know logically didn't matter, but things that still continued creeping in anyway.

She wasn't ready to divulge those thoughts.

Not when she was in a room of happy, smart, beautiful women.

Not when she felt none of those things.

Not when she knew she *should* be feeling all of them because she was so fucking lucky and privileged and—

"The reason you have that look on your face is why I'm not going to answer the question," Rachel murmured, reaching over Sera and squeezing her hand. "What's going on?"

What *was* going on?

So much and yet nothing she could pinpoint.

Annoying and destructive thoughts and yet a wonderful husband and family.

No sleep and feeling like a cow and—

She started crying.

"Oh God," Abby said, wiping frantically at her eyes. "Ignore me. I'm fine. I just—" A sob bubbled up in her throat. "I'm just tired and hormonal."

"Maybe," Bec said, "but it's not *just* that. Otherwise"—she waved a hand in the direction of Abby's face—"you wouldn't look like that."

"Like what?" Abby asked, affronted.

"Miserable," Sera said. "Do you think you have PPD?" she asked. "You got pretty blue after Carter was born."

Abby's first inclination was to immediately deny she felt depressed. Not because it was a negative thing. She knew it was common, and she truly *had* felt very sad after Carter's birth, perhaps even depressed. But Carter had slept better than Emma, and she'd had CeCe around to help.

So maybe it *was* just fatigue.

Maybe she should hire the night nurse like Jordan suggested.

But then she would be doing even less, and the scales would be tipped even more in her favor and . . . she wouldn't be doing anything or enough or—

"I don't think I'm depressed," she murmured, wiping the tears away.

"Then what, honey?" Sera asked. "For all intents and purposes, you have everything you've ever wanted."

Abby stared at her hands. "Then why does it feel as though it's all going to get torn away? Like any second it will be gone, or Jordan will get tired of me and move on, or my kids will get sick or I will, or we'll all get struck by lightning!" She sighed. "I know it's ridiculous," she said. "But every instant of the day, my thoughts are in this cycle. What if Jordan doesn't like my body now? I'm heavier and stretched out and—God—he saw me poop twice on the delivery table. Twice!"

"Abbs," Sera began.

"And I *know* it's ridiculous," she repeated. "Jordan loves me and doesn't care what I look like. But he's a fucking Greek god with a six-pack and I've got a flattened, lumpy *keg!* And—"

"Didn't he used to have the mystical eight-pack?" Heather asked.

A strange question from the man's sister.

Abby blinked and glanced down at the phone. "Um . . . yes?"

"And you don't love him less just because he has two less . . . packs?" Heather asked.

It was such a ridiculous question that Abby just looked at her.

Then eventually answered, when Heather stared back through the screen at her, brow lifted, inscrutable expression in place.

"Of course not," she finally said, albeit a bit mutinously.

"Well, that's that," Heather said, rubbing her hands together. "He loves you, sickeningly, so if he's willingly invited our lot into your place to take over and fuss and eat and drink him out of house and home. And that's just from a friend perspective," she added when Abby began to shake her head. "From a sister perspective, I know I've never seen my brother happier."

"It's true," Sera said. "Even from that first night in the bar, he's never had eyes for anyone but you."

"And," Rachel murmured, "the way he looks at you is . . . right. He's not worried about the varnish on the surface, he loves what's within."

Silence.

Then Bec grinned and shook her head. "Damn Morris, you're good."

Rachel smiled. "It's Scott now, but I'll take it."

"I thought you were going to stay Morris?" Abby asked. Rachel had been married before, to a man who was a special brand of asshole. She'd vowed to never change her name again.

"I've decided I like being a Scott," she said, eyes full of love.

"I bet you do," Bec chortled.

"How's Luke?" Rachel asked innocently.

They all laughed when Bec's—or Becky as Luke called her— cheeks went pink, but she was a true New Yorker and didn't back down, teasing Rachel about Bas and Sera about Tate, and Heather about Clay, just for good measure.

"Also, fuck the notion of having to do it all," she said, turning her laser-sharp focus onto Abby. "That's just some bull-shit patriarchy hangover. Jordan isn't working, but you are, or will be soon. He can definitely pick up the slack. And even if he *was* working and you weren't, you just spent the last nine months puking your guts up and then pushing a watermelon out of something that's the size of a lemon"—here, she shud-dered—"and you've been playing milkmaid with all the nursing and then when you go back to work, I know you'll be pumping. He can do some of the work around here."

"It's more than some."

"So what?" Heather said. "Plus, my brother has never been shy about expressing himself. If it gets too much, he'll tell you."

Abby bit her lip. "He wanted to hire a housekeeper to come in once a week and maybe someone else to do the laundry, but I told him no."

"So no to the night nurse, no to the laundry service—which sounds amazing, by the way—and no to the housekeeper," Sera said, ticking the items off on her fingers. "Why don't you want the extra help?"

"I—" She sighed. "It's just such a waste of money, and I should—"

"And there goes my bullshit meter, scaling right off the charts," Bec said. "Jordan sold off his multi-billion-dollar company a few years ago to sit on a beach. He found you instead and wants to make your life easier."

"But that's just it exactly," Abby said, jumping to her feet. "He wanted to be on a beach and instead, he got me pregnant and now he's saddled—"

She broke off.

Not quite able to finish the statement.

Unfortunately, someone else did.

"Saddled with you," Jordan said from the hall, a bowl of popcorn in his hands and hurt marring his expression. "You think *I* think I'm saddled with you?"

"Oh shit," Heather whispered.

Abby's heart sank. "That's not what—"

"Dad?" Hunter called. "Is the popcorn done?"

He swallowed, glanced up the stairs and smiled. "Just finished. Be right there, but it's probably only one more episode before bed."

"Aw, man!" But his voice faded, his footsteps drifting back down the hall.

"That's not—" She broke off again, took a step toward him, and stopped.

"That's not what you meant?" he asked quietly. "You don't actually think that?" His eyes were hopeful, as if he wished she'd just been spewing nonsense in the heat of the moment and none of it really meant anything.

She wanted that, too.

Except, she couldn't quite bring herself to say that she didn't mean it.

Because deep down, some part of her did wonder if he wished he'd ended up on that beach in the tropics instead of her working for his former company, their home just miles away from what had once been his office, their family growing by the year.

Maybe he wanted mai-tais and margaritas instead of leaking nipples and poopy diapers. Maybe he wanted his freedom instead of being tied to the school calendar and extracurriculars. Maybe he wanted to find someone who wasn't a nerdy, sock-loving, pajama-wearing cow-equivalent.

Maybe he wanted more than her.

And he must have seen those thoughts on her face because he swallowed again, and it looked painful, even from the far side of the room.

"Jordan," she began.

"I should get Hunter the popcorn," he said, lifting the bowl.

She bit her lip but didn't know what to say, how to make him understand this wasn't about him.

It was her.

All her.

He held her gaze for another few seconds then nodded and disappeared. She listened to his footsteps on the stairs, disappearing down the hall, until finally, the bedroom door clicked closed.

"Shit, Abbs," Bec said, breaking the silence that had fallen.

"I know you didn't mean to," Sera whispered, "but I think you hurt his feelings."

Abby *knew* she had, and she felt awful about it. This whole thing was supposed to be about her and her messed-up head. Jordan had been nothing but wonderful and understanding and helpful and . . . now she'd hurt him, made him think that she thought that—

Fuck.

She needed to untangle this mess of thoughts in her mind and go fix things with her husband.

Now.

She went to stand, then realized she was still on her feet, still frozen in place and staring at the empty hallway.

But her friends weren't frozen.

They'd stood too, were gathering up glasses and bowls and

napkins, carrying everything to the kitchen. CeCe began washing up, Sera loading the dishwasher. Bec returned snacks to the pantry, and Rachel had retrieved the re-useable wine stopper and was plunking it in the bottle of pinot grigio they'd opened, before stowing the plugged container in the fridge. In less than five minutes, they had the space spic and span again. Then they were bundling into their coats and slipping out the front door.

"We'll give you some privacy so you guys can talk," CeCe said, pulling her in for a quick hug.

"It'll be okay," Rachel murmured, hugging her after CeCe had slipped by.

Bec kissed her on the cheek. "Just talk to him," she said. "He's a good guy. He'll understand where your head is." Then she tugged lightly on the end of Abby's ponytail and walked down the path to the driveway.

Sera stopped on the threshold, weaving their fingers together and squeezing lightly. "Honey."

"I hurt him," Abby whispered. "He's been the perfect fucking husband, and I just hurt him."

"I think you need to talk about exactly why that hurt him so much—"

"I—"

"Not with me," she said, not unkindly. "With him. Because you two are the product of some pretty messed-up families. Not that mine is anything to write home about," she added. "Because God knows, my parents are a special brand of dysfunctional."

"I don't think this is about our childhoods."

Or maybe it was. Shit. This had just gotten so infinitely complicated.

Sera smiled, touched her cheek. "I think you just realized that maybe this is deeper than you first thought."

Abby sighed, nodded. "I think you're right."

"I know I am," Sera said lightly. "But, babe, what you need

to think about more than my all-knowing rightness is whether you're actually worried that Jordan is unhappy *or* if this has more to do with your dad's special track record of making new families every couple of years."

Abby sucked in a breath.

Fuck.

Fuck.

Because if Abby's dad was bad about using women like tissue and discarding them just as easily, then Jordan's dad was even worse.

And if part of her was worried, however stupid and illogical she knew that was—even in her emotional, hormonal state— that she might end up like one of those tissues . . .

Then Jordan must think that *she* thought he was like his father.

And that might be the worst insult she could ever give him.

CHAPTER SIX

Jordan

HE WAS PRETENDING TO SLEEP.

Like a child.

Lying in bed, the popcorn propped on his chest, next to his son, and pretending to drift off.

Because he knew that Abby was going to come up.

Her friends were too intuitive to not have recognized the wound his wife had unintentionally—and he knew it was unintentional because she was too damned nice to hurt him on purpose—but they were too smart to stick around after that.

And sure enough, he had barely made it to the bedroom before he'd heard the footsteps and the dishes clattering then the front door opening and goodbyes being given.

Then fifteen minutes later, footsteps on the stairs and Abby had crawled into bed.

Luckily, he'd begun his fake sleeping already, so Hunter had just whispered loudly—*loudly* because it seemed like no matter how kids tried to lower the volume of their voices, it was still ear-piercing, "Dad's sleeping!"

"I see that," came Abby's lilting voice, at a much more

reasonable volume. The bed shifted as she crawled onto the mattress. "Can I join you for the last little bit of this episode? It's one of my favorites."

"It's epic!" Hunter said over a certain not-quite-Jedi wielding her saber.

"It is at that," she whispered.

And Jordan didn't chime in.

Because he was pretending to be asleep.

Pretty soon the episode was over, and Abby left with Hunter to tuck him into bed, but when she returned, he immediately knew the jig was up.

Mostly because she sat down next to him on the bed and said, "I know you're awake."

He stifled a sigh but opened his eyes. "Hey, sweetheart, you ready for bed?"

She just looked at him.

He just looked at her.

And then she released a deep breath and said, "I know I hurt you, and I'm sorry."

She had, but it hadn't been on purpose. He knew that. But he'd been so convinced he could just easily fix this little bump in the road she was having if only he took enough off her plate and got her some sleep and time with her friends. He never considered that the real issue would be . . . her worrying he would leave her.

Some part of her honestly thought he would leave her.

Like his father.

Like *her* father.

Fuck, but that stung.

But it wasn't like either of them had great examples of men in their lives. It wasn't a surprise that there would be some deep-seated anxiety and fears. Or that she would be especially vulnerable during times like these, when she was exhausted and there were all sorts of hormones flowing through her.

It was just . . .

He wasn't his father.

He knew that. *She* knew that.

So, he didn't need to make it even harder for her.

Shifting, he slipped an arm around her waist and tugged her close, taking solace in the feel of his wife near him while shoving the slice of pain away.

"I know, baby," he said. "It's okay."

She sighed, her arm coming around him. "It's *not*."

"You said something in the heat of the moment," he told her, running his hand up and down her back. "I'm not hurt."

He wasn't hurt.

Not really.

It was the fatigue talking. For both of them.

Soon things would settle down and they'd be back to normal and he wouldn't feel like this, like he'd been scoured from the inside out. He would be totally fine and it wasn't a big deal and—

"Don't lie to me, Jor," she said, sitting up enough for him to see her face.

He brushed a finger over her lips. "What's that they say about eavesdroppers?" He forced himself to smile. "That they won't like what they hear? I'm fine, sweetheart," he added lightly, needing her to know that it was . . . and it would be. But more than that, he knew he didn't need to add his hurt feelings to her burden. Especially when it would all be fine. He'd get over it. "Though what's *not* fine is you thinking that your body isn't beautiful."

A roll of her eyes. "It's hard to feel beautiful when you're a cow."

Opening his mouth to protest, he didn't manage to actually get that protest out before she covered his lips with a finger.

"That's not in the sense of I'm fat and disgusting—though I won't lie and say that I love all the new stretch marks and sagging bits, especially when you seem to only grow more handsome as the years go by—but I feel like a cow with all the feedings. No"—a shake of her head—"not just *that*. It's this sense of my body not being my own, like I'm standing in front of the mirror and seeing someone else."

He squeezed her arm. "You've had a lot of changes since we got married. Getting pregnant with Carter and becoming an instant mom to Hunter, the new job, another baby. I feel like that would throw anyone for a loop."

"But it's not like you haven't had any changes."

"Don't you see?" He sat up, tugging her up with him, heart full of so much love for her. "I didn't start actually living my life until I saw you in that bar. I'm so thankful to have you, to have our family, our kids, even your friends."

Her eyes went damp. "I'm so thankful to have you, too. I love you so much. It's just . . ."

"Just what?" he pressed when she just trailed off.

"Just"—she bit her lip—"I just worry that you want that beach."

He snorted, thinking of how delusional he'd been, selling his business, buying an island—an actual island. Jordan had wanted privacy and quiet, or so he'd thought. Because he knew himself well enough now to recognize that he would have been absolutely miserable.

"This life I have with you . . . it's more than I could have ever imagined. I wake up every morning feeling so fucking lucky to be next to you."

She sniffed. "Even if it's being woken up at three A.M.?"

"Even if it's being woken up at three A.M. paired with the sounds of a child vomiting."

They both shuddered, remembering the worst throwing up incident of their marriage. At least, he figured she was remembering the same thing as him—avocado exorcist a la Carter.

"Even if your wife says something unforgivable?"

"Even if my wife is obsessing over something that isn't a big deal," he said, deliberately meeting her eyes. He believed the statement, too, even if it still smarted, because it wouldn't be a big deal.

At some point, it wouldn't be a big deal.

He knew it.

He just needed to . . . something. He needed to get some sleep, let some time pass, and the pieces would settle into place.

And it wouldn't hurt so much.

And part of him would stop worrying that deep down he was like their fathers.

Because he wouldn't let that happen, *couldn't* let that happen. Not when he had so much. Not when he knew the worth of having Abby and Hunter and Carter and Emma in his life. Not when they both had so much more than the men who'd contributed half of their DNA to them. Jordan knew the worth of that, of the family they'd built, and wouldn't ever take it for granted.

"I love you," she whispered, hugging him tight.

"I love you," he whispered back. "Come on," he said, coaxing her down next to him, "let's sleep before Emma decides she's up to party."

Abby giggled but curled up into him. "I shouldn't be tired," she murmured, resting her head on his shoulder. "I had two naps"—a yawn interrupted her statement—"today."

"Sleep, sweetheart."

And after a few moments, she did.

But he lay awake, turning her words over in his head, wondering how he could make her see that he wasn't ever going to leave her.

Wondering how she could even think that when he felt so tied to her, to their life.

Wondering how he had gone his whole life thinking he was so different, but even his wife was worried that he was the same as them.

Sleep stayed out of reach, her words clawing into him, the barbs locking in deep.

And he continued to wonder.

As the sun rose, dawning on a new day, he hadn't gotten any closer to the answers. Instead, he just wondered how he was going to prove to her—and perhaps to him as well—that he wasn't like their fathers.

CHAPTER SEVEN

Abby

SHE'D FUCKED UP.

Yup.

She'd known it from the moment she'd seen Jordan's face but had relaxed after their talk that night. He'd seemed to understand, had promised he wasn't hurt.

But now, as the week had gone on, she knew he was a big old liar.

He *was* hurt, and he was trying to prove that he wasn't.

The reality of what she'd said, what she was feeling, how she'd so hurt the man she loved had prompted her into action the next day. So she had called her doctor and made an appointment. They'd discussed her emotions and insecurities and fatigue and had agreed that if she still felt so unsettled the next week, she would try some antidepressants and meet with a therapist.

But her words had been the catalyst that yanked her out of the fog.

Well, that and the sleep. And the fact that she'd finally had enough energy to start going to the gym. With all of those things, she was finally thinking clearly and feeling better and not so caught up in her own head and insecurities to not see the rest of the world around her.

Slowly but surely, she was feeling more like herself.

Still, she'd kept the therapist's number. Just in case she started feeling so twisted up again and needed more help.

But while she was starting to feel more like herself, he was on edge, something fragile about his emotions, even as she tried to show him that she knew he wasn't like his father, that her freak-out had been about her and not him.

And they were both doing it without really talking to the other.

Oh, they *were* talking.

About everything except the giant fluorescent pink elephant thundering beneath the surface—Carter and his new words, Emma and the fact that she was actually sleeping thanks to Jordan's insistence on giving her that late-night bottle, on Hunter capturing the lead in his class's play as Professor Rock, oh and the new nanny they'd interviewed based on CeCe's recommendation who would be starting in a few days.

Everything was settling in, calming down.

And yet, nothing was.

Because her husband was hurt, even though he was putting on a great front.

Abby sighed and pushed off the chair in the back yard where she'd been enjoying the feel of the afternoon sunshine. She knew that she needed to figure out a way to take back those words.

Or not take back, she supposed, since she knew that was impossible. Instead, she needed Jordan to know that she knew that he wasn't like their fathers. But, fuck, just thinking that tangled line of thoughts was confusing, let alone trying to prove something just so someone else could let go of their biggest insecurity wasn't easy.

As a woman who'd spent nearly all of the last two months

in that cycle of self-doubt and uncertainty, she knew one conversation couldn't break it.

She'd needed Jordan and her friends, then the blow of seeing his face, then talking with her doctor, followed by several nights of thinking and journaling, and then several more conversations with the Sextant to get her head on straight.

Oh, and she'd needed sleep, too. And the gym.

Because all those pieces together had finally unsnarled the tangle.

Or maybe rather than untangling, she'd passed the snare from her to Jordan, like some perverse game of emotional telepathy.

He was sitting at the kitchen counter, his laptop open, a file from Heather open on the screen that he was reviewing for her. But his eyes were shadowed, and when he heard her come in, he jumped up and crossed to her. "Hi, sweetheart," he murmured, tugging her close and giving her a peck on the lips. "Need anything?"

"No, thank you, baby," she said, squeezing him back. "I'm just going to start dinner."

"It's already in the oven."

She froze. "I told you it was my turn."

"I was here and knew the recipe."

"Jor—"

He hesitated, uncertainty on his face, and she hated that she'd made him doubt himself. "Yeah, sweetheart?"

Which was why she said, "Thank you" instead of anything else.

And then the same later, when he ran her a bath and rushed to gather up the kids so she could have private time—definitely much-appreciated, aside from the thread of vulnerability in his eyes, the slightly-desperate tone of his voice.

But it was his expression this morning that made her shift her thinking from this would pass—that it would just take some time to convince him she didn't think of him as his father or hers, for that matter—to recognizing this wasn't just going to fade away. She could be as patient as possible, could keep trying to reassure him that she knew the difference between him and their dads, but he wasn't going to absorb that.

Because she'd hit at his greatest vulnerability.

And that wasn't something that was easily erased.

Luckily, she had an idea.

CHAPTER EIGHT

Jordan

THE KIDS WERE ASLEEP.

And so was his wife.

But he was sitting at the kitchen table, putting the finishing touches on the file for Heather and wondering if he'd done enough over the last couple of weeks to prove to Abby that he was in for the long haul or if he needed to do more.

Did she know?

Did she feel how desperate he was to keep her? To prove to her he had staying power?

He hoped for the first, not for the second two. No man wanted to be seen as desperate, and certainly not by the woman he was desperate for.

At least, he thought that should be the case.

But it was becoming harder and harder to not just tell her that he was still thinking about what she'd said, that it was affecting him still, that he wanted her to know that—

Ping.

An email hit his inbox, his eyes flashing to the corner and seeing that it was a message from . . .

Abby?

"Uh," he muttered, not particularly eloquently, but his fingers moved over the trackpad, and he clicked on the message anyway.

Jordan,

I know I hurt you. I've seen it in your eyes, even though you've tried to pretend everything is fine. Take it from someone who has plenty of experience pretending, none of that will make any difference. It will keep eating at you, keep making your thoughts all twisted up and impossible to let go.

But I was lucky enough to have a husband who understands and cares and loves me unconditionally, friends who push me to get my own head out of my ass, and a wonderful family I feel absolutely privileged to be a part of.

And yet, I know that sometimes all of those things don't make a difference.

Sometimes your mind won't let you out of that tangle.

So, I've decided to yank you out myself—with a journey. ;)

Hopefully by the end, with all the evidence, you will see you are not like them. I hope you will see all you mean to me, how much I love you, how strongly you've <u>stitched</u> yourself into the fabric of my soul. Forever.

That's your first clue. Now here's your second.

You started with a chain, then a slip, and a single and a double.

—Your love,

A

He sat for a moment, staring in wonder at the email, reading it through again, and feeling his heart squeeze tight.

He hadn't been fooling her, not for a moment, had he?

Just as she hadn't fooled him with all of her "I'm fine" nonsense.

Jordan hadn't been able to sit back and watch her zombie-ing through life all uncertain and lost. Just as she, apparently, couldn't stand to watch him unravel. Stubborn, the both of them, but also stubborn in the best way.

God, he loved this woman.

And he knew exactly where the first clue was leading him.

He closed his computer and walked into the family room, heading for the basket she used to keep by the couch, but was now kept on one of the built-in shelves.

Tucked in between two skeins—see? He *had* learned something from his wife's crochet lessons—of yarn, was a small folded piece of paper with his name written on the outside in Abby's messy handwriting.

Your clue is a wall we created out of love, one that I insisted upon, but one that you insisted was laid out in crisp, even perfection. Every time I look at it, I feel my heart grow full at what we've made.

His gaze flew up, locking onto the wall where Abby had nixed hanging his favorite painting and instead insisted upon hanging family pictures when they'd moved into this house. It had begun small—starting with just the two of them, then the addition of Hunter, then adding Abby's pregnant belly, then Carter, then another pregnant belly, and then . . . a new addition that hadn't been there earlier in the day.

The five of them gathered together on the couch, Hunter tickling Carter, Abby holding Emma, who was smiling, and him, his face turned toward his family, love shining brightly in his expression.

His heart thumped.

Then he walked over and grasped the slip of paper tucked under one corner of the picture.

I love you and our family, more than words can express.
For your next clue, go peek in on our newest and find her favorite lovey.

He smiled and quietly went up the stairs.

Then just as quietly, he slipped into Emma's room, moving to the ugly stuffed dog that had once been Abby's childhood toy and was now Emma's absolute favorite thing to stare at. Currently, it occupied the rocking chair, another slip of paper folded underneath its right foot.

He opened it.

Our littlest is trouble, just like her mama, but I know you love us both very much. Now, for your next clue, find little squishie's favorite book, and further that, his favorite page. :)

Jordan tiptoed over to the crib, brushing a soft finger over Emma's nose. She frowned, just like her mom did when he touched her while she was sleeping. Laughing softly, he left her room, walked down the hall, and moved into Carter's room.

Who was passed out in his toddler bed, his butt stuck in the air, same as he'd slept since he'd been able to roll onto his belly to get into that position.

Navigating the stuffed animals and books and Duplos littering the floor, Jordan went to the bookcase and pulled out *Goodnight Moon*.

"And a comb and a brush and a bowl full of mush," he whispered to himself, opening up to Carter's page, heart thudding when his fingers brushed another slip of paper.

I knew you'd find it because you're a great father, because you pay attention to the details. You always remember the important things, and we are so lucky to have you. Now before I cry (damned hormones!), you'll find your next clue in the last-minute project you ran out to get supplies for.

He'd known it was coming, that logic told him he'd be next journeying to Hunter's room. But, considering he'd been cursing to himself about having to craft a mission out of popsicle sticks and craft glue only hours before, this made him smile.

After quietly closing the door behind him, he moved to his oldest son's room, heart expanding with love when he saw the mini-me of his brother sacked out on top of the covers, a book open on his chest. Such a voracious reader, just like Abby was. And . . . just like Zach had been. Though he missed his brother intensely, Jordan knew he was beyond lucky to have Hunter in his life.

Carefully, he put a bookmark in to keep Hunter's place—he'd lived with bookworms long enough to not make that mistake—set the book aside and tugged the covers up and over his son.

Then he moved over to the dreaded mission project to read the note propped up outside its front door.

If you were like our dads, you wouldn't have known about my crocheting or the photos. If you were like your or my father, you wouldn't have known about the lovely or the favorite page in the book or Hunter's last-minute project. If you were like them, you wouldn't know where to find me now.
So for your final clue, your wife will be in her favorite place.
The one you made so special for her.

"Fuck, but I love you, Abby," he whispered, pocketing the note, and continuing down the hall. Past their bedroom and into the small study that he'd converted into a reading nook.

White shelves stacked high with books. A comfy chair with colorful throw pillows and fluffy blankets. A space heater because the blanket was never enough.

And his wife.

Sitting on that chair, with a fuzzy throw covering her, a book in her lap.

In her favorite pajamas, cozy socks on the feet sticking out from beneath the blanket.

She set the book aside. "Hi," she whispered.

His heart was full. "Hi, baby," he said, crossing over to her. "How—" He broke off, not knowing what to say except, "I love you."

Her eyes were gentle. "I love you, too. I'm sorry if I didn't show that to you before, or at least not how I *should* have." She brushed her fingers over his jaw. "I'm sorry I hurt you."

He took those fingers in his, squeezed lightly. "Honey, don't say that. I'm fine. I—"

"*Jordan*." Her voice was firm. "Don't sweep this under the rug. I hurt you."

He started to shake his head, then stopped, knowing he owed them both the truth. "Okay, I *was* hurt. I felt . . ." A sigh, but she was silent. "I think part of me has always worried I'll turn out like them, even though I know exactly how valuable our life is."

"But you're not like them." She took his hand, squeezed it. "And I'm so sorry that I made you think that."

"It's o—"

"Not okay," she said sternly. "Certainly not okay. But I'll do what it takes to prove to you that my insecurity was about me, about my childhood baggage, and had nothing to do with you."

His heart was full, that jagged cut not nearly so painful. Because of the notes and the journey, because of the love and care in her eyes, her touch, her words. He cupped her cheek. "I'm familiar with baggage, childhood and otherwise, but it's so much easier to bear knowing I have you and the kids. You make my life full. And the notes . . . baby . . . the things you said." His voice cracked, but he pushed on. "I don't think I've ever felt more loved or appreciated, and I want you to feel that same way, to be secure that I'm not going to leave you like our fathers did, trading wives and families like baseball cards." He brushed her hair back from her face. "I want you to know that I'm here for the long haul and don't care what you look like or how many kids are running around our house or whether or not I have to go out for wood glue. I love *you*. The person you are inside. The person you've helped me become. The family we've built. The—" His throat went tight, words stoppering up at the top of it. "I just love you," he finished, not too poetically, but it was the truth.

And probably the most important truth.

"I love you, too," she said, lips curved into a soft smile. "Throughout these last couple of weeks, I realized I was living in comparisons." A shrug. "I know that doesn't make much sense, but basically I was comparing my body to how it looked before kids, comparing the things we're not doing with what we used to do, comparing everything I felt for you and how much it has changed. And it *is* different." She bit her lip. "I was worried that because my love felt different from a few years ago, it meant yours did too and that it would mean your passion would fade or that you would eventually want something different."

"Abbs—"

"But now I understand my mind, my feelings better," she said, squeezing his hand. "We're not in the first bloom of love, we're in the *forest* of it. We're the tall trees growing up to the sky, the flowers sprouting beneath, the animals and critters weaving and running in between. Clearly, I'm not one for poetry." A laugh as she shook her head. "But suffice to say, I've realized comparing our life now to how it had once been without thinking of how much it has expanded is unacceptable. It may be different, but for all the differences, it's so fucking incredible that sometimes I feel like I'm at risk of waking up from the best dream ever. Because"—she leaned forward, brushed her lips across his—"I have you and Hunter and Carter and Emma and my nosy friends, and we've made our own family that's not in the shadow of what we grew up in. It's fully in the sunshine and it's wonderful."

"Fuck, sweetheart," he groaned, the words broken, tears dangerously close to spilling over. "You're killing me."

"Good," she whispered, "because I'm about to kill you some more." And with a wicked smile, she shimmied out of her pajama pants then undid the first button of her top, then the next and the next and the next, until she was clad in only a silken black negligée. "I've decided to love my body for the cow it is"—her smile turned mischievous as she brought his hand to her breast—"but I might need you to remind me of that every once in a while."

"Once in a while?" he rasped.

"Yes," she said, arching into his touch. "And also right now."

Then she kissed him, slipping her tongue into his mouth, love and passion and desire mixing together until he broke apart to pay gentle homage to those glorious breasts, until he'd skimmed his fingers over the soft curve of her belly, the gentle slopes of her thighs.

"Get me naked, baby," she whispered, squirming against him, against the light strokes of his fingers.

"In a minute." Another stroke that made her gasp. One more that made her groan. Then he slid the straps from her shoulders, tugged it off her body, and showed her exactly how much he loved her body—stroking her naked skin, kissing his way down her torso, licking her between her thighs. He pulled out every last trick he knew.

"Oh God!" she moaned, gripping his shoulders, tugging him down over her. "Enough, Jor. I want you inside."

Since that was where he wanted to be too, he made short work of removing his clothes, crawled back onto that big chair, and then slid inside.

"Yes," she groaned, holding him close. "God, I've missed this."

He was too close to the edge to risk any words. Instead, he concentrated on gaining control and not blowing his load. And then he concentrated on bringing her to that edge with him.

Then beyond it.

Thank fuck, she made it over the precipice.

Because in the next second, he exploded, pleasure flooding him for an eternity, before he collapsed on top of her, barely having the presence of mind to roll to the side so he didn't crush her, as he caught his breath.

Long minutes later, she stiffened in his arms.

"Sweetheart?" he asked.

"Please, tell me we didn't just make baby number four," she said, eyes wide.

Because . . . birth control. *Right*. They hadn't worried about that much over the last years of pregnancy.

"Shit," he whispered.

But then her lips curved, her arms wrapped around him, and her mouth found his, laughing as she broke away and shook her head. "Well, if we hop aboard that train, I'm glad I have you with me."

"First-class cabin all the way."

And as they both laughed, Jordan hugged her tight, knowing that truer words had never been spoken.

He was so glad to have her with him.

BILLIONAIRE'S CLUB

Bad Night Stand

Bad Breakup

Bad Husband

Bad Hookup

Bad Divorce

Bad Fiancé

Bad Boyfriend

Bad Blind Date

Bad Wedding

Bad Engagement

Bad Bridesmaid

Bad Swipe

―――――

Hate missing Elise's new releases? Love contests, exclusive excerpts and giveaways?

Then signup for Elise's newsletter here!

http://eepurl.com/bdnmEj

―――――

BILLIONAIRE'S CLUB

Did you miss any of the other Billionaire's Club books? Check out excerpts from the series below or find the full series at www.amazon.com/gp/product/B07JVRRGCT

———

Bad Night Stand
Book One
www.books2read.com/BadNightStand

Abby

"I'M THE BEST FRIEND," I said and lifted my chin, forcing my words to be matter-of-fact. I'd been through this before. "You might be fuckable to the nth degree and perfect for Seraphina, but I refuse to set her up with a liar."

In a movement too quick for my brain to process, my stool was shoved to the side and I was pinned against the bar, heavy hips pressing into me, a hard chest two inches from my mouth.

Seraphina whipped around at the movement and I could just see her over Jordan's shoulder, her blue eyes concerned.

"Hi, Seraphina, I'm Jordan," he said, calm as can be, gaze locked onto my face then my eyes when mine invariably couldn't stay away. "I'm going to borrow your friend for a minute."

"Abs?" she asked, and I knew she'd go to bat for me right then and there if I needed her to.

"Weasel or no?" I managed to gasp out. For some reason, I couldn't catch my breath.

Not that it had anything to do with Jordan.

No, it had *everything* to do with him.

"Weasel?" he asked.

I shook my head, focused on my best friend. Weasel was our code name for the men trying to weasel, quite literally, their way into my pants and then into hers.

I was just about ready to say fuck it—or me, rather—even if Jordan was a Weasel. He smelled amazing. His body was hard and hot against mine.

And it had been way too long since I'd had sex.

"No chemistry on my part—" Seraphina began.

"Your friend isn't who I'm attracted to," Jordan growled out. "You are, and it's fucking pissing me off that you don't believe that."

———

Bad Breakup
Book Two
www.books2read.com/BadBreakup

CeCe

"You're even more beautiful than I remember," he said, and the rough edges of his accent hacked at the words, making them more of a growl rather than a soft sentiment.

Her breath caught, and she found her eyes drawn to the

stormy blue of Colin's.

And she stared again, utterly entranced before she remembered how it had all ended.

Her in a white dress.

Alone, except for the priest who'd given her a pitying look and invited her to stay as long as she needed.

But it had always been like this, Colin's gruff words winning her over. They were unexpected from him—he was typically so reserved and taciturn. And that compliment, freely given as it was, chipped away at any defenses she managed to erect.

The problem was that his words weren't always followed up by action. In fact, they were typically trailed by pain for her and fury for him.

The hurt of those memories—of Colin so angry, her so broken—helped shore up her resolve.

"Don't say things like that," she snapped and started to pop her earbuds back in. Her friends at home had filled her phone with a slew of romantic audiobooks and she decided that she much preferred fictional heroes at the moment.

At least if they broke their heroine's heart, it was only once.

Colin had already broken hers twice.

She wasn't looking for a round three.

—Get your copy at www.books2read.com/BadBreakup.

———

Bad Husband
Book Three
www.books2read.com/BadHusband

Heather

"I'm getting drunk," he said, but allowed her to pull him inside the car so that her driver could shut the door behind them.

"You're already drunk," she said.

He stiffened. "*More* drunk."

"Fine," she said, half-worried he was going to launch himself from the sedan. She'd never seen Clay like this. Usually he was so cold and uncompromising, impenetrable even under the toughest of negotiations. He was . . . well, he was typically as *Steele*-like as his last name decreed.

She wrapped her arm through his in order to prevent any unplanned exits from the vehicle and gave the driver the name of her favorite bar. "If you really want to drink, let's do it right."

And *then* she'd drop him at his hotel.

Except it didn't happen that way.

Yes, they hit the bar.

Yes, they drank.

Yes, they got plastered.

But then they woke up . . . or at least, *Heather* woke up.

Naked.

With a softly snoring Clay Steele passed out next to her in bed.

That wasn't the worst part.

Because Heather woke up naked and with a softly snoring Clay Steele in her bed *and* she was wearing a giant diamond ring on her left hand.

Still not the worst part.

That came in the form of a slightly crumpled marriage certificate tucked under her right cheek.

And not the one on her face.

She pulled it from beneath her, a cold sweat breaking out on her body, dread in every nerve and cell.

She *still* wasn't prepared for the horror she found.

The marriage license had been signed by . . . Heather O'Keith and Clay Steele.

Holy fuck, what had she done?

—Get your copy at www.books2read.com/BadHusband.

———

Bad Hookup
Book Four
www.books2read.com/BadHookup

Rachel

The man didn't take the hint. He didn't leave.

Why won't he leave?

She dropped her chin to her chest.

"So," he finally said after another lengthy—and silent—moment. "Gay, taken, or not interested?"

"Oh my God," she moaned, one hand coming up to push her bangs off her forehead. "This is *not* happening."

"I—" A beat then his voice was incredulous. "I *know* that moan." Warm fingers grasped her wrist, tugged until she could see him in all his yumminess.

Her moment of weakness. Her hookup because she'd been feeling desperate and lonely and—

"It's you," he said softly.

Yes, it was *her*. Rachel, the good girl who didn't sleep around, who *certainly* didn't hook up with random strangers in a bar.

Rachel, who *had* hooked up with a stranger.

The sex had been damned good. Incredible, actually.

But it had been just that. Sex. And she hadn't been able to let go of the guilt. She'd now slept with a grand total of two men in her life, and one of them was her husband.

"I—" She tugged at her wrist. "I need to go."

—Get your copy at books2read.com/BadHookup.

––––––––

Bad Divorce
Book Five
www.books2read.com/BadDivorce

Bec

Bec really didn't expect to see another person waiting for her when the doors opened with a soft *ding* and she stepped off.

But there *was* another person waiting just outside her front door.

A person she never expected to see again.

Luke Pearson.

Her ex-husband.

It was one-fucking-thirty in the morning, and her ex-husband was sitting on the floor outside her apartment.

Asleep.

Fuming, she marched over to him and kicked his shoe. Hard.

"Luke. Why in the ever loving fuck are you here?"

His lids peeled back and sleepy green eyes met hers. "Becky," he murmured. "You're gorgeous as always." The drowsiness began to fade from his expression. "Did you just come from work?" He glanced down at his phone. "Do you know what time it is?"

"Of course I know what time it is—" Bec bit back the words. Fuck, but wasn't this conversation an exact replica of the broken record one they'd had *way* too many times over the course of their relationship?

She crossed her arms. "Never mind that." A glare that had withered balls much bigger than Luke's "Why did you break into my apartment?"

He stood. "First, I didn't break into your apartment. This is the hall. Second," he hurried to say when she opened her mouth to argue semantics, "I didn't break in. You used our anniversary as the code."

Oh for fuck's sake.

Well, she was changing that tomorrow . . . today . . . fuck, *yesterday*, now that—

"Go away, Luke," she said, pushing past him and unlocking

her door while blocking his view of the keypad that was identical to that of the elevator. Her front door's code was not the date of her anniversary with her ex.

But Luke probably already knew that, given that he had been sitting on the floor of her hallway rather than on her couch, beer in hand, feet making prints on her glass coffee table.

Men.

Fucking men.

She slammed the door closed behind her and threw the dead bolt. The knock approximately one second later did not surprise her. Bec dropped her briefcase to the floor then opened it just enough to shoot angry eyes at him through the narrow gap the dead bolt allowed.

Serious green eyes fixed onto hers. "We need to talk."

"Luke," she snapped. "I'm exhausted. It's the middle of the night. I wouldn't have any patience to talk to my best friends right now, let alone my ex-husband."

"Funny story about that," he said, his lips curving. "Turns out that I'm not actually your *ex*-husband."

—Get your copy at www.books2read.com/BadDivorce

———

Bad Fiancé
Book Six
www.books2read.com/BadFiance

Seraphina

Sera was alone, pining after a man who'd created the latest social media craze.

Yup. Her life was *ah-maz-ing*.

Tate cleared his throat, and Sera realized she'd been staring at him dumbfounded for a good couple of minutes.

"How can I help you today?" she asked. "I do hope"—*Do*

hope? What was she, British? *Ugh.*—"I-uh . . . I hope you were able to find a house. The agents I passed along are very good at finding unique properties, and I even gave them a few locations to start with . . . " She bit her lip, attempting to stop the ramble.

"No."

Just no.

Um. Okay.

He lifted a hand, rubbed the back of his neck. The movement made his shirt lift, exposing several inches of flat stomach and tan skin and, oh God, a trail of blond hair leading south. Her mouth watered, desperate to trace that path with her tongue—

Sera sucked in a breath, popped to her feet.

"Ah. I'm sorry." She picked up a random file, pretending to know what was in it. "I'm actually really busy, so this will have to continue another time."

Like never.

She rounded her desk, forced a smile. "Mr. Conner," she said when he didn't move. "I'll have my assistant schedule something soon."

"Seraphina."

She shivered at the sound of her name on his lips—soft, a little raspy, and deep enough to conjure all sorts of unhelpful fantasies in her mind.

Shaking herself, she moved to open the door.

Suddenly, Tate was there, hand on hers, body inches away, spicy scent inundating her senses.

Sera's breath caught. "What are you—?"

He seemed to be arguing with himself then finally, those piercing blue eyes locked onto hers. "I need you to marry me."

—Get your copy at www.books2read.com/BadFiance

ALSO BY ELISE FABER

Breakers Hockey (all stand alone)
Broken (May 24th, 2021)

KTS Series
Fire and Ice (Hurt Anthology, stand alone)
Riding The Edge
Crossing The Line (March 22nd, 2021)
Leveling The Field (June 14th, 2021)

Love, Action, Camera (all stand alone)
Dotted Line
Action Shot
Close-Up
End Scene
Meet Cute (April 5th, 2021)

Love After Midnight (all stand alone)
Rum And Notes
Virgin Daiquiri
On The Rocks
Sex On The Seats (April 26th, 2021)

Life Sucks Series (all stand alone)
Train Wreck
Hot Mess
Dumpster Fire
Clusterf*@k (August 16th, 2021)

Roosevelt Ranch Series (all stand alone, series complete)
Disaster at Roosevelt Ranch
Heartbreak at Roosevelt Ranch
Collision at Roosevelt Ranch

Regret at Roosevelt Ranch

Desire at Roosevelt Ranch

Phoenix Series **(read in order)**

Phoenix Rising

Dark Phoenix

Phoenix Freed

Phoenix: LexTal Chronicles **(rereleasing soon, stand alone, Phoenix world)**

From Ashes

In Flames

To Smoke (October 18th, 2021)

Stand Alones

Someday, Maybe (YA)

ABOUT THE AUTHOR

USA Today bestselling author, Elise Faber, loves chocolate, Star Wars, Harry Potter, and hockey (the order depending on the day and how well her team -- the Sharks! -- are playing). She and her husband also play as much hockey as they can squeeze into their schedules, so much so that their typical date night is spent on the ice. Elise changes her hair color more often than some people change their socks, loves sparkly things, and is the mom to two exuberant boys. She lives in Northern California. Connect with her in her Facebook group, the Fabinators or find more information about her books at www.elisefaber.com.

f facebook.com/elisefaberauthor

a amazon.com/author/elisefaber

BB bookbub.com/profile/elise-faber

O instagram.com/elisefaber

g goodreads.com/elisefaber

p pinterest.com/elisefaberwrite